# RETURN TO ATEN

## The Second Chronicle of Aten

Lynn Sinclair

Brown Barn Books
Weston, Connecticut

Brown Barn Books
A division of Pictures of Record, Inc.
119 Kettle Creek Road, Weston, CT 06883, U.S.A.
*www.brownbarnbooks.com*

Return to Aten

Original paperback edition

Library of Congress Control Number 2005935279

ISBN: 0-9768126-0-6
        978-0-9768126-0-6

Sinclair, Lynn
RETURN TO ATEN

Printed in the United States of America

# Dedication

To all housecats who dream of having an adventure.

# Acknowledgements

Thanks to my daughter, Shelby, for the brainstorming sessions (and sharing the computer); Yuki for believing; Mom, Dad, Deb and Steve for opening their doors; Patti Hunt and Sandi LeFaucheur for never hesitating to dive in; fellow Backspace members for their wit and wisdom; Nancy Hammerslough for making a fantasy a reality; Barb Hibbitt, Erika Willaert and librarians Reccia Mandlecorn and Margaret Fleming for cheering me on; all the helpful folks at PGC; Barb Anderson and Audrey Allman for saying yes; Blake Edwards for making my website shine; and my family and friends for their continued support and encouragement. And, of course my cat, Chowder, for insisting she be included in the book.

# Chapter One

D*ear Gramps*

*I'm leaving. No, not running away (although living with Mom isn't easy), I'm running to something—the future. I know it'll be hard to believe, but what I'm about to write is true.*

*Generations from now, Earth will be called Aten and civilization as we know it will come to an end. I don't know how or when it's going to happen, but I'm going back to find out.*

*A group of women, called the Nera, will be sent from somewhere (another planet, I think) to help what's left of our society. Their offspring will have special abilities. One guy, Caden, has a voice that can make people and things do whatever he wants. His half-brother, Aladar, has power over plants. Apparently, I have a special ability too. Don't know what it is, but that's just one of the many questions I need to answer.*

*There's a hidden archive filled with information and treasures from our time. I didn't have enough time to check it out, but it's obvious, because of all the things stashed away, that someone knew what was going to happen to Earth. Those are the good things. Unfortunately, there's lots of bad stuff, too.*

*Like the Hachi. Gramps, you haven't seen a spider till you've seen these guys—they're as big as basketballs. And the Chuma. Let's just*

*say you don't want to be around these people when they're hungry. I
don't even like to think about them.*

I laid down my pen and rubbed my eyes, but no amount of
rubbing could erase the memory of the chalky-faced Chuma I'd
killed in self-defense. I took a deep breath and picked up the pen
once again.

*The worst person is the Major—he's huge and to be honest, terrify-
ing. He controls Holo, a filthy place where the people of Aten trade
what little they have. The Major wanted me to open the archive (oh
yeah, I forgot to tell you that I have the key to the archive).*

I clasped the silver snake charm hanging from a chain around
my neck. Enrial, the Nera's leader, said I had a job to do: *"Return
to Aten, take your rightful place and help get this world back on track"*.
Although I'd only recently found the charm, it was no coincidence—Enrial had chosen me long ago and only now felt I was
ready. Was I?

*Even with all those terrible things, I have to go back to Aten. My
best friend, Neil Moran (you remember him? He lives down the street),
is still there with his dad. They were able to travel to the future through
their dreams and, like me, the people on Aten consider them 'outsiders'.
I hope they're okay.*

I stared through the kitchen window and into the darkness
beyond. Only hours before, I'd left Neil, Mr. Moran and
Aladar trapped by the Major on Aten. Had they been able to
escape?

*And I may as well tell you everything about Caden. Even though
he's only eighteen, he's chief of the Dani tribe and he's amazing. In fact,
Caden's the best thing about Aten.*

*You're probably shaking your head and already making plans to fly
back to save your insane, sixteen-year-old granddaughter. I won't be
here. I'll try to visit, but I'm not sure I can come home. I don't under-*

2

*stand everything; I only know I've got to return to Aten. I don't care about the dangers (well, maybe a little).*

*I love you, Gramps, you've always been there for me. Please don't worry.*

*Love, Jodi*

*p.s. I've left a note for Mom telling her I was going to try and find Dad. Don't tell her the truth, but take care of her for me, okay?*

I folded the slip of paper, pressed my fingers along the crease then slipped it into an envelope. I hesitated before sliding my tongue over the gummy flap. While searching through the junk in the kitchen drawer for a stamp, I heard a creak on the floor-boards over my head and froze.

"Jodi, what are you doing up?" My mom's voice echoed from the upstairs hall.

I didn't want to answer, but was snagged by guilt. Ever since my dad had abandoned us when I was five, Mom had gone downhill. For the past few years, she'd seldom come out of her drunken stupor long enough to be a real mom. Now I was abandoning her too.

"I couldn't sleep, so I came down for some milk." I glanced at the shorts and T-shirt I wore. "I'll be up in a sec."

"It's after one and there's some things I need you to do tomorrow."

What would Mom do when she woke up to find me gone? What would she do without me?

"Sure, Mom." I saw a stamp poking up through all the pens, tape and abandoned receipts. With a quick lick, I pasted it onto the corner of the envelope, propped the letter against the toaster and walked to the bottom of the stairs. Mom hovered at the top, the hall light illuminating her sleep-tossed hair.

"You're not even in your pajamas. Did you just get in?" she asked.

Her face was hidden by shadows, but I could imagine the suspicion in her eyes. I grasped the banister and pulled myself up the stairs. Her housecoat was stained even though I'd washed it a few days before, and I saw a new hole where she'd burned it with a cigarette.

"Don't worry, Mom." I touched her arm. "I'm almost done."

She shrugged my hand away, turned and shuffled toward her bedroom.

"Mom?"

She looked back at me, her fingers resting on the doorknob.

"I love you." How long had it been since I'd said that?

For a moment, the haze lifted from her eyes and she nodded before slipping past the door and shutting it behind her. Sighing, I returned to the kitchen, put on my jacket and grabbed the bulging knapsack with a sleeping bag hanging from one of the straps. I was almost out the door before remembering the letter to Gramps. I grabbed it and then followed my cat, Chowder, onto the porch steps. Without glancing my way, she sauntered toward the sidewalk, her tail whisking back and forth as though waving a wand.

"Does this mean you're coming to Aten with me?" My voice was loud on the otherwise silent street.

I patted the mailbox after slipping the letter inside. "Bye, Gramps."

Not wanting to take the chance of any neighbors seeing me suddenly disappear, I strode into the dark forest at the end of our street. I had a flashlight in my knapsack but decided I knew the paths well enough. When I reached the towering oak tree where Neil and I had once built a tree fort, I stopped.

Chowder executed a figure eight around my ankles and I picked her up before grasping the charm in my hand. Enrial had hinted I could return to Aten without Neil's help, and I was sure the necklace would get me there.

My heart thumped like a tribal drum. Was I doing the right thing? Was there really a place for me on Aten? I closed my eyes and envisioned Caden's village—neat, dirt roads lined with log houses and sweet smelling gardens. That's where I wanted to go. I curled my fingers around the charm. The ground sucked me in, wrapping damp earth around my ankles, then my legs. Chowder was crushed against me as we sank into the muck. Neil had been right; I'd gotten used to the once terrifying trip. A damp breeze and harsh smell of smoke replaced the eerie silence of my forest. I opened my eyes.

# Chapter Two

Broken log gates dangled, framing Caden's village, Ganodu, smoldering within. Blackened walls rose from the ground and sizzling wood hissed. A light rain misted from the gray sky, too little and too late to stop the damage.

Chowder dropped from my arms as I stared at the once proud home of the Dani tribe. A thousand thoughts raced through my head. Obviously a battle had been fought but with whom? Caden's crazed uncle, Arax, had killed Kalone, leader of the Millit. Had that tribe attacked Ganodu? I hitched my thumbs through the straps of my knapsack. I'd seen a lot of brutality and death when I'd been on Aten but didn't know if I was prepared to see what had happened to these kind people.

I wrinkled my nose at the invisible tendrils of smoke that wove through the rain. The place was a dying campfire, wet and forgotten. The village had been leveled, the houses nearly destroyed and the once colorful gardens were now just smudges of paint on a black canvas. I leaned against the gatepost before dragging my feet inside. Chowder held back, seeming just as unwilling to enter.

"Hello?" I was almost afraid someone would answer.

I jumped when a chunk of timber fell from the walkway that ran along the top of the walls circling the village. The wood crashed into a puddle, splashing cold, muddy water on my legs.

I looked back through the ruined gates at the trees—gold and red, crisp and dying, the leaves drifted to the ground. I'd been back in my own time for less than twelve hours, yet it was now fall on Aten—months must have passed since I'd last been here.

There was nothing for me in this village. I turned and ran, calling to Chowder. The trees had laid a slippery layer of leaves on the road leading from Ganodu and my feet skated apart. I landed on my butt and, not caring about the dampness beneath me, I pressed my forehead against my upraised knees. I'd been so sure Caden would be here, that someone would be here. So sure of my importance to Aten, I'd bounded into the future with a knapsack full of hopes. Chowder paced beside me then stopped and stared through the mist, her ears flattened against her wet fur.

The sound of careful footsteps came from the dense forest beside us. I pushed up from the ground and dashed to the other side of the road, away from the approaching steps. As I neared the first tree, something sliced past my ear and embedded itself in the hard wood. An arrow. I stopped and reached for my necklace, then remembered Chowder. Knowing I'd be safer anywhere else, I still couldn't leave without her. I licked my lips.

"Don't move." A man's voice.

Move? I hadn't even considered it; the arrow had been enough to slow me down. I took a breath and turned.

"What's your business here?" Wearing the suede pants, jacket and boots of the Dani tribe, the man with shoulder length, black hair narrowed his eyes. "You're the one Caden called Jodi."

I nodded, relief lapping at my frayed nerves.

"Come with me." He tugged the arrow from the tree and headed back into the woods on the far side of the road.

"What's happened to Ganodu?" I ran to catch up. "Where's Caden?"

"I think it obvious what's happened to our village. As to Caden's whereabouts, no one knows."

He pushed a willow branch out of the way and it flapped back, spraying my face with drops of water while Chowder dodged beside us, along a path of her own. I smelled smoke—not the same as the burning village, this smoke carried the promise of warmth and food. The man parted the thick branches of a prickly pine tree and we stepped into a clearing.

A dozen people jumped from their tree stump seats when they saw us. All women, they were in the midst of stirring pots over several small fires or sewing together animal skins that lay across their laps. Children's voices filtered from the surrounding forest—carefree shrieks and laughter that seemed to echo from a different world. Horses, with blazing white coats, huddled in a small corral, and a girl, with long, damp hair clinging to her shoulders appeared from behind them. Catta.

"So you've finally returned," Catta said as she approached.

The last time I'd seen her, she'd been hanging possessively to Caden's arm, claiming she'd make sure he forgot all about me. Had she been successful? It was obvious from the way her lip curled that I wasn't a welcome sight.

"I found her near the village."

"She's the reason Caden isn't here to protect and lead us." Catta pointed at me.

"Where is Caden?" I asked.

"Gone, taken because of you," Catta said.

"What have I to do with it?"

"What have I to do with it?" Catta mimicked me in a whiney voice. "You've everything to do with it. While you were safe in your hiding place, the Major swooped in here looking for you. He took Caden instead."

"But Caden could easily escape, couldn't he?" I said. "He only needs to use his voice."

The other women gathered around, smelling musty as though they'd been left in the rain far too long. I closed my fist around the strap of my knapsack.

"He barricaded Caden in an invisible box," said the man who'd found me.

I imagined Caden imprisoned by the Major's force field, the same one I believed he'd used on me. The Dani's fire no longer smelled promising or warm.

"The Major was looking for you or, rather, something you had." Catta stepped toward me. "He'd be very grateful if we delivered that something to him."

Someone grabbed my arms as Catta reached out and pulled the necklace over my head.

"No! You can't give that to him," I said. "Caden wouldn't want you to."

"Oh, I think Caden's probably had enough of life inside his invisible box. And we need him here." The snake charm swung back and forth as Catta held it triumphantly in the air. "I think we've found the answer to our problems."

"If you give the Major this key, he'll have access to the archive and to information that will help him take over everything on Aten," I said. "You can't let him near it."

"And Caden was so sure you loved him. Won't he be surprised to learn you didn't want to set him free."

I pulled my arms loose and attempted to snatch the necklace from Catta, but she held it above her head and laughed. Someone grabbed my hands again and pinned them behind my back.

"Tie her up," Catta said.

"But she's Caden's friend," said the man.

"She's no friend." Catta planted her hands on her hips. "Do you think our village would be lying in ruins if not for her? Would all our people be away searching for Caden if it weren't for her? While the Dani spend their lives striving for progress, she comes here and destroys all we've worked for. Caden was deceived by her lies, but I can see right through them."

"Please, don't believe her, it was the Major who did this to you, not me," I said.

The faces surrounding me turned away. Cloth bit into my wrists, trapping the knapsack against my back, and I struggled even though I knew there was nothing I could do.

"Ramen," Catta said to the man who had found me, "I'll take this necklace to Holo and free my husband, but first, we'll have to decide what to do with her."

She folded the necklace in her hand, then stuffed it into a beaded leather pouch hanging from her neck. She narrowed her eyes and smiled at me. "Yes, you heard me right. My husband."

I spotted Chowder in the lower branches of a tree, her tail flicking from side to side in rhythm with my thoughts—husband, husband, husband. A whoosh of air sounded behind me before something hard hit the back of my neck.

A million mosquitoes were humming in my ear while an elephant stood on my head. I reached out for the sleepy place I'd been, but it kept ducking from my grasp. I opened my eyes, my lids like sandpaper, while my hand, squashed beneath my hip, sent signals that I'd been in this position a long time. I pulled it free, relieved it wasn't tied, and shook out the tingling sensation. Sitting up, I tried to ignore the imaginary elephant that wouldn't go away.

I was surrounded by sand, white and glaring under the sun, and spindly trees dotting dunes that rose and fell like the tracks of a roller coaster. My clothes were covered in mud, dried into the creases. I raised my T-shirt to my nose—eau de horse.

Alone. What had happened to Chowder? Hadn't she been able to keep up with the horse they'd obviously carried me on? Had she even tried? For some reason, I'd thought she was meant to be my companion here on Aten, but she was, after all, simply a cat. My cat. I should've left her at home where she'd be safe. What if she wandered under the shrouded trees of the Hachi? I pressed my knuckles against my lips and tried to blot out the picture of Chowder wrapped in a gigantic spider's web. No, no, I couldn't think like that. She'd be safe with the Dani; they were kind people, most of them anyway. I wiped tears from my face. I'd go back for Chowder as soon as I could.

I unzipped my knapsack, amazed they'd not taken it from me. I was even more surprised to be alive, but as much as Catta may have wished I didn't exist, I didn't believe she'd stoop to murder. She probably hoped I'd admit defeat and crawl under a rock somewhere. Catta didn't know me very well.

Then I remembered Catta had called Caden her husband. Had Caden given up hope of me ever returning and married her instead? Had he only pretended to love me? A weight pressed against my chest and I slammed my fist on my knee. How could he have done this to me? After taking a few deep breaths, I brushed the sand from my legs. She'd lied, plain and simple. All I had to do was retrieve the necklace and find Caden.

I dug into the knapsack, pulled out a bottle of water and Gramps' handy pocketknife. I slipped the knife into my jacket pocket then drank half the bottle of water before remembering I'd only brought two. Better ration because I had no idea when I could refill them. Picking at the label, I gazed around.

This could be the same Drylands I'd come through with Caden, Neil and Aladar after the battle in Nereen where we'd defeated the Major and his gray-clad soldiers. The sun was directly overhead and, if I kept an eye on where it traveled, I'd know which way was east. Would that help me? I shrugged, deciding I'd head away from the setting sun and hope it would lead me to the Awes' forest where Aladar lived. If Aladar lived.

The water had chased the elephant on my head away and I rummaged in the knapsack once more for my sunglasses and 'Save the Dolphins' cap. The sun had moved a bit in the sky, showing me the way east. I stood, ignoring the discomfort of the sand that had worked its way into my underwear, and sucked in a breeze that was tinged with a hint of autumn. I'd have to put on my jeans before the day was through. Placing one foot in front of the other, I shut out the repeated chorus in my head: husband, husband, husband.

Thirst gnawed at my throat and my shoulders ached where the knapsack rubbed against them. The weight of all the baggage was slowing me down, so I decided to take only what I needed and leave the rest. I changed into my jeans, hooked the sleeping bag over my shoulder and stuck a full water bottle in my jacket pocket. After hiding the knapsack behind a lone rock, I continued on, my feet dragging through the soft, shifting sand.

I'd been determined not to look at my watch, but the sun didn't lie—it was embedded in the horizon behind me, a half disk of blazing red that was leaving me to the night. I peeked down at my wrist, shocked to discover I'd been walking for over five hours and the landscape hadn't changed. It was time to stop.

I laid out my sleeping bag and slipped between the warm covers. It smelled of mildew and fires, conjuring up visions of Gramps and I camping—he'd linger over the embers as I snuggled down for bed. I missed him and, if I were completely honest, I was scared being alone in this place. I dug into my jacket pocket for one of the granola bars I'd brought and took my time over each crunchy mouthful. When I was done, I balled up the wrapper and tossed it on the ground beside me. I felt guilty about littering, so I reached out in the dark and, scrambling around for it, felt something soft; something that didn't belong there. My stomach flipped. As though in slow motion, I bent my neck and peered into the night. A quiet, unnerving chuckle sounded from the shadow hovering over me.

"Look what we have here, boys." Arax, Caden's uncle, bent down and yanked me from the safety of my sleeping bag.

# Chapter Three

I'd last seen Arax, his face contorted with rage, when Caden had replaced him as chief of the Dani tribe. Now he smiled, a grin that tore his face in half. Five men, standing behind Arax, nodded their heads, eyes like dark pits in their faces. And even in the feeble light of the moon, there was no disguising the chalk-covered bodies of the Chuma. Would their memory be as clear as my own? They closed in around me, their thin fingers stretching out, poking my arms and chest. I pressed against Arax.

"No, no, she's not our dinner tonight." Arax backed this up with a vigorous shake of his head. "We won't dine on such a valuable morsel. At least, not yet."

The Chuma's arms dropped to their sides.

"So has Caden tired of you already?" Arax asked.

"What are you doing here?" I asked.

"It's refreshing to hear human speech, instead of the grunting of these," he lowered his voice and sneered at the Chuma, "fools. They understand well enough but seem incapable of actually forming the words. Nonetheless, they do take direction well."

"So you're leading the Chuma now?"

He hiked up his baggy, suede pants. "Admittedly, it's not as illustrious as ruling the Dani but it does have its benefits, though the choice of food isn't one of them."

I shivered, folded my hands into my pockets and felt Gramps' knife. The night enveloped us in semi-darkness and if there was somewhere to escape, I couldn't see it.

"What are you going to do with me?"

"You're a valuable commodity these days and I'm in need of something to trade. Seems we're starting all over again, doesn't it?"

"I'm of no use to you, Arax, I don't have what the Major is looking for anymore."

"Ah, the necklace." He frowned. "Had I known its worth, I'd have taken it and killed you long ago. Where is it?"

"Catta's taking it to the Major." I slapped my hand over my mouth then shrugged away the information as though it were unimportant. "You may as well leave me here to die, I can't help you."

"Get your bedding, you're coming with us."

It was too late to grab my sleeping bag—one of the Chuma pranced about with it wrapped around his shoulders while the others giggled and tugged on the zipper. The young man wearing it stopped and all of them gathered around, running the zipper up and down. I'd never get the sleeping bag back.

"I don't know what would give me more enjoyment, handing you over to the Major or watching the Chuma carry you off to…you don't want to dwell on that, do you?"

Arax was too greedy to give up any promise of a reward, but I still felt sick knowing he had the power to make that decision. As much as I hated him, he was the only thing stopping the Chuma from serving me up on a platter.

"Where are we going?" I asked.

"If the necklace is on its way to Holo, then so are we. It's lucky I found you, well, not so lucky for you. You're quite popular around here—everyone is looking for sweet, priceless

Jodi, and the Major is willing to pay an astounding amount of goods for your capture. Considering I lost everything because of you, it's only fitting you should be instrumental in getting it back."

"You lost everything because of your obsession with the Conjurer." I could still remember the astonishment on Neil's face when he discovered that the man on Aten known as the Conjurer and rumored to hold the secrets to progress was his own father who had been missing for over three years.

"Funny, that." Arax's laugh had a surprised sound as though he wasn't used to finding humor in himself. "I would've traded you for that useless outsider, when all along, you were the one."

My mind and body screamed with exhaustion, but if I fell asleep, I was sure the Chuma would find a way of stealing me from Arax and taking me back to the Pass; the place that seemed to be the starting point for every mistake I'd made since I'd first come to Aten.

"Where are we?" I asked.

"The Drylands," Arax said. "We'll reach the Pass by morning."

"I'm tired, I don't think I can keep going all night." I needed time to think of a way to escape.

"We could stop and rest." Arax stroked his chin. "If we do, I'd advise you to sleep with one eye open because they've missed many meals."

Every part of me was numb with fear. I reached up for the charm and its comforting coolness before remembering it was gone. Why was Arax the one who'd found me? How could anyone have found me in this vast desert?

The air was cold and my breath came out in small, smoky puffs. I stuffed my shaking fists up the sleeves of my jacket and concentrated on lifting each foot out of the sand, one after the other. I thought of my mom, curled up in her bed and probably so warm, she'd tossed the blankets aside. If I were home right now, I'd crawl in with her like I had only a few years ago after a nightmare. Everything had been so right back then. My chin dropped and I closed my eyes as I followed behind Arax. There would be no warmth for me tonight.

My back itched where the sweat trickled down my spine. I struggled with my jacket, rolling over and taking in a mouthful of sand. Jumping up, I squinted in the bright sun and spun around, searching for the Chuma. They lay, huddled in a pile like a bunch of old rags while, all around us, the desert spun on forever. I turned, looking for a lifeline, but there was only Arax, hugging his knees beside a dying fire. He seemed smaller than the last time I'd been on Aten; shrunken and sagging.

"Your nap has cost us time." He got up and kicked at the pile of rags. "Let's get moving."

The Chuma groaned and stretched before getting up and wiping the sand from their chalky arms. They stared at Arax, their eyes narrowed, and I wondered how long it would be before they tired of his leadership. I hoped I wouldn't be around to find out.

"My partner's waiting for me on the other side of the Pass," Arax said.

Partner? What idiot would put his trust in Arax?

"Then we'll get rid of these fools," Arax continued. "They're useful, but I'm beginning to question their loyalty."

"Who will the great Arax lead then?"

His hand whipped out and smacked my face. I covered the sting with my palm as the Chuma laughed.

"You're braver than when we first met. I like it." Arax raised his hand and I flinched as he ran his fingers over my hair, getting them caught in the curls. "Such unusual, auburn hair. It's unfortunate we'll soon be parting ways."

I fondled the knife in my pocket. If only I'd woken during the night as the Chuma slept, I might have been able to use the knife and escape. I unclenched my fist and the knife dropped back into the deep folds of my pocket. No, no matter how much I hated Arax, I could never kill him. I stared at Arax's back as he turned away and hate welled up inside me. Oh, but how I'd like to make him disappear forever.

Arax tripped and sprawled out in front of me. He rolled over and glared at the Chuma, who grinned and pointed at him. Getting up, he strode over to me and grabbed my arm.

"You do that one more time and I will give you to the Chuma."

"I didn't do anything."

He pushed me in front. "Get moving."

If Arax had someone waiting for him on the other side of the Pass, I'd never have a chance to get away. But we'd have to get through the Pass first and I had a sickening feeling that the Chuma had other plans for us. I glanced warily at them and one of the Chuma grinned, his teeth even and white. I slipped off my jacket and tied it around my waist, knotting the sleeves twice

As the morning progressed, the landscape slowly changed. Instead of sandy dunes, long, dry grass sprouted, crunching under our marching feet. I licked my lips, wondering where my bottle of water had disappeared.

"Drink this." Arax passed a leather flask to me. "You might be able to stomach it."

Any liquid was better than none and I downed a few gulps. It smelled like rotten eggs and tasted worse, but I was thankful for it. As I lowered the flask, I spied the Jagger Hills, stretching across the horizon. The wide fissure of the Chuma Pass, visible far in the distance, was the quickest way through the rocky hills. My mouth went dry again and I took another sip of the rancid water. Perhaps this was what I deserved; to die in the very place I'd killed another Chuma.

The smiling Chuma with us now picked up speed and tugged on my arms, motioning me toward their rocky home. The shadows on the high, rocky hills shifted. Arax seemed intent on ignoring the Chuma's antics, perhaps rethinking his own plans while our companions grunted their special brand of language. I wanted to close my eyes to the haunting sight of the Pass but was afraid to take my gaze off the Chuma. Didn't Arax realize what was happening?

As we neared the hills, the sound of the wind whistling through rocks drifted over the meadow. There were no Dani to fight off the Chuma this time and even if I were willing to use it, my insignificant knife wouldn't get me through safely. My knees trembled and I stopped walking. The Chuma turned and grasped my arms.

"Get away from her," Arax said.

It was too late. The Chuma dove on us.

"Why did you bring us this way?" I gasped and pulled away from their rough fingers. Looking up, I saw the hills come alive with chalky forms.

Arax dodged to the side, but two of the Chuma piled on top of him barking and grunting as they twisted his arms. Arax roared and threw them to the ground, but like puppies, they tackled his legs and nipped at his calves. Then all activity stopped as a thunderous noise filled the air. I glanced into the hills then over my shoulder where dust swirled in the distance, heading our way.

Six horses, pulling two chariots, burst through the cloud and sped toward us. I didn't care if the devil himself was holding the reins; I tugged away from the stunned Chuma and ran toward the newcomers.

The wheels shot dirt in every direction and the horses whinnied and reared as they were pulled to a halt. Sprinting toward them, I glanced behind me and saw the Chuma only meters away. I pushed forward.

Two men in long, black coats jumped down from the chariots' platforms, each twirling something above their heads. They threw their arms forward and the sun's rays caught on several shiny objects zipping toward me. I dove to the ground and the Chuma stumbled over me as the missiles hit the ground. The Chuma screamed and I heard their footsteps speeding away toward the hills.

I was sure the beating of my heart was making a sizable dent in the earth as I lay flat on the dry grass, waiting for another, more accurate shot. Flecks of dust floated around me then someone grabbed the back of my shirt and turned me over. I swiped my hand across my eyes.

"Aladar!" Even as I said it, I knew he wasn't Aladar, Master of the Awes forest and a man who had proven himself to be my friend. Yet they looked almost identical. Long, fair hair and elegant features, but their eyes, though both a silvery gray, were different. Whereas Aladar's constantly danced with mischief, his seemed guarded and grave.

"No."

"You look…"

"Just like him." He squatted down and peered at me. "And who might you be?"

"Jodi."

"The infamous Jodi." He gripped my hand.

Tiny, electrical currents ran down the inside of my arm. His gray eyes widened and we stared at one another.

"This is interesting." He pulled me up before releasing me.

I looked down at my hand and arm, sure there would be burns from the sensation I'd felt, but there was nothing.

"We'd better get moving, the Chuma haven't admitted defeat," he said.

I twirled around and, sure enough, the Chuma had gathered their forces once again. Arax ran in front, looking frantic and shouting, "Wait!" above the rampage.

"Into the cart, now!" The guy in the black coat hesitated and then grabbed the empty sleeve of my jacket and dragged me to safety.

Arax leapt onto the other chariot, grappling with the other driver. Aladar's almost-twin pulled me onto the platform before hooking his long fingers around a bird's nest of reins and giving them a shake. Seeing his friend in trouble, my driver pulled out his large slingshot and hurled a sharp silver stone toward the other chariot. It found its mark and Arax slumped to the floor.

"Shall we drop him somewhere?" He picked up the reins again and the horses bounded away.

"Who are you?" I gripped the side of the chariot.

"The finder of lost possessions." He kicked at my knapsack on the floor, never taking his gaze from the road ahead. "Does this belong to you?"

I reached down, pulled the knapsack to my chest with one hand and, closing my eyes, breathed in its familiar scent.

"I see that it does. When I found it, I was surprised to see the condition of the artifacts inside."

"Where I come from, this knapsack and everything in it is the latest design," I said.

"Here, on Aten, they're relics of another time."

My throat constricted. Everything and everyone I knew were gone, long turned to dust. Without the necklace, I had no way of going back home and suddenly I wanted to go back very badly.

"You didn't answer my question. Who are you?"

"My name is Rad."

"Are you related to Aladar?"

"He's my brother." He signaled to the other man and they both pulled on the reins, slowing the horses to a gentle walk. "Have you seen him lately?"

"He was battling the Major's soldiers the last time I saw him, although I don't know how long ago that was. In fact, I was hoping to find Aladar." I fell against the chariot's side as it bumped over a dune and landed on a broken strip of old highway. Arax's feet hung over the edge of the other platform, his toes dragging on the ground.

"You're hiding from the Major?" Rad asked.

"Does everybody know he's looking for me?" I hadn't seen any telephones around here, but the people of Aten seemed to have quite the communication system nonetheless. "No, I need help finding the Major because he has something I want."

Rad laughed. "He'll find that amusing as he's under the impression you have something he wants. Perhaps you can trade?"

I shook my head and explained what had happened to the necklace and Caden. A tiny piece of my brain wondered why I trusted this stranger, yet the words flowed out of me, happy to find a home.

"So I have to find Caden before Catta takes the necklace to Holo."

"Amazing that one girl could potentially bring down our world," Rad said.

I silently agreed wholeheartedly before realizing that he may have been speaking about me.

"You mean Catta?"

Rad smiled but didn't say anything. The landscape changed as we headed back into the Drylands. Minutes, then hours, passed by in silence. Every once in awhile my eyes closed and my chin dropped into my chest, but I'd be jerked awake by a bump or turn.

"We're almost home," Rad said.

Up ahead, the ground erupted with shadows that, like every-thing else on Aten were familiar yet different. As we neared, buildings, pitted and crumbling, came into view. The town or small city, it didn't matter which, was long dead.

# Chapter Four

The floor of the one-story building was clean and a breeze grazed the room, lightly touching the few pieces of ancient furniture. Maybe it had once been an office or a restaurant, but now most of the window frames were boarded up and the others, open to the elements, allowed sunlight to beam across the uneven, concrete floor. A man and woman sat at a rusted metal table surrounded by mismatched chairs in various states of disrepair. Rad stood in the center of the room, his black coat falling in deep folds around him. He looked so much like Aladar, my fingers ached to reach out and touch him.

"She can't stay here," the woman said. Her short, spiky, blond hair looked as though she'd chopped it off in the dark. "The Major'll be on us within the flick of a bat's wing."

"Then what do you suggest we do with her, Stala?" Rad asked.

"With every greedy searcher on her trail, the best thing to do would be to take her back where you found her." Stala sniffed. "She'll ruin us."

"That won't happen," Rad said.

The other man, his thin face sprouting several days' worth of gray whiskers, lifted his head and stared at Rad. "We've needed your insight many times before, yet you've been unwilling to give it. Seems odd you'd provide it now."

Rad stepped to the empty window, his dark silhouette casting a long shadow across the room. Finally, he turned, his face hard. "There are some truths even I can't ignore, Paul. It doesn't matter, we can't toss her back out there."

"What about Arax? We owe him nothing," Stala said. "I think it would be wise to drop him as far away from here as possible."

"I agree." Paul turned to me. "Would you like to go with him?"

"With Arax? No thanks." I tried to keep my voice steady but whether from hunger or fear, it leaked out in a tiny whimper.

"It seems Arax is determined to give you to the Major and I won't play into his schemes. We'll keep him locked up for the time being and give you a head start," Rad said. "Until then, why not rest here?"

I dropped my knapsack on the table. My forehead pounded and I pressed my fingers against my closed eyes. A hand, surging with current, gripped my arm and, feeling a chair at the back of my knees, I collapsed into it. I heard murmuring, not catching the words, and a woman's angry voice bit through the haze. My lips became numb, my mouth dry and I pitched toward the floor, my head suddenly too heavy to sit atop my shoulders.

*There is no such thing as time travel.*

These words rumbled in my head as I stared skyward through steel beams that crisscrossed the nonexistent ceiling. There was no such thing as time travel, and Caden wasn't married. Could both those things be true?

The sun shone in a cloudless sky that looked as though it had been smeared with a brush dripping in blue paint. I squinted and the makings of an atomic-sized headache nibbled at my brain; I needed to eat. I sat up and checked out my surroundings. No longer in the room with the table and chairs, this space was the size of a classroom with a thin layer of straw coating the floor. Dried and bleached by the sun, the straw made me think of bees buzzing and hot days sipping lemonade. I pushed up from the floor.

No one else was around and the only sound was the rasp of my feet on the straw as I walked through a hole where a wall might have once stood and looked out onto a house-tall pile of brick. Sure there was no such thing as time travel.

I wandered along what must have once been a street. Eerie. Most of the heaps of rubble had become tiny islands of nature where grass, weeds and scrubby bushes grew over the past. Huge black birds soared above me, swooping and rising on air currents I couldn't feel below. A chinking sounded from ahead; tiny, whispering taps. I hesitated for a moment then decided I knew only one way of finding food and that was through other people. Around the next bend, a man and woman dug into a grassy hill with long handled spades. Wide-brimmed straw hats sheltered them from the sun.

"Careful there, Stala, don't strike too deep."

"We hardly need to worry about taking a chunk out of the brick, we've got enough of that stuff to last a lifetime." She swept her arm around, jerking to a stop when she noticed me standing below. "She's awake."

The man pushed back his hat, revealing a pink, sweaty dent along his forehead. It was the man Rad had called Paul.

"So there you are." Paul dropped his spade and worked his way down the hill, feet sliding out from under him a couple of times. Reaching the bottom, he placed his hand on my shoulder. "Come with me."

Stala huffed, tugged on the brim of her hat and shoved her spade into the dirt again. We stepped over debris, went around a few more corners and came to an area cleared of the dismal reminder of a ruined city. Planks of wood teetering on top of small brick columns served as tables and benches where several groups of people sat, heads bent close together over the remains of their meals. The hum of their conversation stopped as they watched us approach. Paul greeted them and guided me to a buffet laid out on a table beneath a cloth canopy.

"Not much left this late in the morning," he said.

Pita-like bread, creamy toppings and soggy vegetables lined up in bowls and on platters. I picked up a chipped plate and a wooden spoon, still coated with the stuff it had last been dipped in, and smeared a white topping over a pita. I nudged Paul aside as I reached for a bowl of what looked like chopped red peppers. Shuffling down the table, I piled on food until the pita looked like a wedding cake.

"Hungry?" he asked.

We sat at an empty table, away from the others. After taking a bite, energy surged through my body and each new mouthful nibbled away at my headache. Paul got up and came back with a plastic cup. I drank the warm water, took a few more bites of food then picked up the cup once more. It felt good in my hand, the plastic rough and nicked in places, yet comforting all the same.

"This is from my time," I said, trying to talk around the food in my mouth.

"Our time."

"You're an outsider, too? I should've guessed by your name."

He nodded. "I came here five years ago, though there's only a few of us on Aten who still use years to measure time. I was determined to make a difference to our future."

"And have you?" I lifted the bottom of my T-shirt to wipe my mouth, remembered how dirty it was and, unable to see a cloth or napkin, used the back of my hand instead.

Paul traced his finger around a knot in the wooden tabletop. "One day I'll make a difference, I'm certain of it."

Would that be me in five years, still hoping to change the world?

"What do you do here?" I asked.

"We dig, we uncover, we find lost things." He smiled. "And when I know, I tell them what the heck everything was used for."

"Is there much left, other than plastic cups?"

"I used to hate how we seemed to make everything out of plastic, an environmental nightmare, or so I thought. Now I'm glad these things have defied the passage of time. Not only do they come in handy," he pointed to my cup, "they remind me of who I was and where I came from so long ago."

"How long do you think it's been since..." I stared at the bottom of the empty cup, "since the destruction happened?"

"I figure it happened about three hundred years ago, but that's just a guess. We've uncovered things that didn't exist in my lifetime, so I've no idea exactly when Earth was destroyed. A lot of what we find, we trade and some of it we keep in storage." He gazed at the other tables. "The folks who live here are different from most on Aten; they believe in preserving the past and their history. I'll show you our museum when you finish up here."

"Where do I put this?" I lifted the plate and looked around.

"Into the bucket, there." Paul pointed to an overflowing tub of dirty dishes and pushed his thin frame away from the table. "I'm in no rush to get back to Stala. She's in a foul mood today. Let's take a stroll down memory lane."

Paul led me along the narrow streets, some crowded with people chipping away at some artifacts of history, others lonely and silent, waiting to be rediscovered. A few smaller buildings had remained intact, at least to a degree, but most were shells, unable to hide their advanced age.

"This place, where are we?" I asked

"They call it Kopi. In Arizona or Nevada as far as I can determine, but I've never ventured far. Might be on another continent for all I know, but it is our world. Once I met up with this group, I decided this was where I could make my biggest contribution."

"Over here." Paul led the way up a narrow path toward a low building that appeared to have survived the devastation. "Each room is devoted to specific finds—appliances in one, tools in another."

The shuttered windows were open and the door, obviously not the original, looked like a hodge-podge of welded metal squares.

"We use whatever we can." He smoothed his hand over the door's rusted and pitted surface. "How long has it been since you've been home?"

"Only a couple of days, though it seems like more."

"You're in for a surprise." Paul swung the door open and stood aside. "Welcome back to the twenty-first century, Jodi."

One time, my mom had asked me to get a carton of old clothes from the basement. Boxes, piled on top of each other in a dark corner, sagged under the weight of their contents. Opening one, I'd breathed in the dust and dampness of forgotten belongings—old, unused, moldy. The memory came flooding back as I stood in the foyer of the ancient building.

"Over here are all the things you might find in a kitchen." Paul opened another door and led the way into a small room where sunlight streamed through the windows. "Most of the stuff we keep is broken but usable."

Shelves, tables and the floor showcased dishes, utensils, pots and, oddly enough, a bowl of fridge magnets. Circling the room, I stopped at a stack of dusty platters, swiped my hand across the surface of the top one and revealed the picture of a turkey. A family may have used this platter for their holiday dinner, probably only bringing it out once a year. Treasured, it had outlived both the family members and their dreams.

"This is all so sad." I rubbed my hand on my pants and turned away.

"It's a bit overwhelming. I'm sorry, I should've warned you." Paul led me back into the foyer. "We'll leave this for another day."

"There won't be any more days, I've got to leave."

"You'd be safer here."

"I won't be safe anywhere on Aten if I don't find..." I stopped and pressed my lips together.

"Oh, the necklace. Rad told us about that. I'd dearly love to see this archive of yours." Paul leaned forward, his fingers folding over my arm. "I could go with you."

I pulled away from his grasp and shook my head. "I have to go to Holo."

"I don't seem to be making much of a mark here. Maybe I can make a difference on Aten if I go with you."

I pushed open the door, stepped outside and sucked in the fresh air. "Do you know the way there?"

"We'd only need a map," he said.

I followed behind Paul, keeping my gaze on the rutted path.

"Rad said you'd seen his older brother, Aladar."

"I didn't know Aladar had a brother." Why hadn't he mentioned it? "Do you know him?"

"Never met him and Rad rarely speaks of him. Are they alike?" Paul asked.

"They look the same. Aladar is," I paused. How could anyone describe him? "arrogant, brave, wise, fun, demanding and generous, all at once. He loves to play practical jokes and, I swear, one day it'll get him into trouble. Even then, I think he could handle anything."

Although I'd eaten only an hour before, my stomach felt as though it had been hollowed out with a spoon. How good it would be to see Aladar, Master of the Awes' Forest, waiting around the next corner; the perpetual glint in his eyes was enough to make me smile. I stopped, mid-stride, astonished that it was Aladar's wisdom I hungered for and not Caden's arms. I walked on again, slower.

"And what are you two up to?"

I glanced up. Rad leaned against a brick column, cleaning his nails with a knife. Gramps' knife.

"Where did you find that?" I asked.

"This?" He held the knife in front of his face as though seeing it for the first time. "On the ground, is it yours?"

I snapped it from his hand, receiving a tiny, electrical shock for my trouble.

"I've been showing her the museum." Paul hesitated. "Jodi wants me to take her to Holo."

I stared at Paul. He seemed awfully eager to come with me.

"Do you know the way?" Rad asked.

"No, but you could map it out for us, couldn't you?"

"I could," Rad said. "Weren't you working with Stala this morning?"

"Suppose I should be getting back." Paul cast quick glances at Rad then me. "I'll see you at dinner."

"He wouldn't be of much help to you," Rad said after Paul left. "An interesting companion, but not much of a guide."

"Is there anyone here who can take me to Holo?"

"There is, but whether they'd be willing to tear themselves away from their work is another question." Rad pushed away from the column. "Did you enjoy the museum?"

"Depressing to know all that stuff belonged to people who are gone now."

"I've always thought of it as a way of bringing them back to life," he said. "But, you're right, it's better out here."

Kopi depressed me. As dreary as Holo had been, this place smacked me in the face with the truth of Earth's destruction.

"Catta might already be on her way to Holo. I've got to get there before she does."

"You must've gotten on famously with my brother; he's another one who expects everything done before it needs doing."

"If the Major gets the necklace, he gets everything." I followed him down the path.

"So you've said."

"It's true." How could I make him understand that the loss of the necklace would affect all life on Aten? "Do you know where my knapsack is?"

"Back in the room where you decided to go for your nap."

Gritting my teeth, I asked, "Could you show me, please?"

Rad chose a different path than the one Paul had brought me along. This one curved around the bottom of a tall, grassy hill and, shielding my eyes against the sun, I looked up. Tall windmills, their blades turning lazily, dotted the top.

"What are those?" I asked.

"One source of our power."

"Wind power? What do you use it for?"

"We've just recently started it up. Unfortunately, we lack a way to store the energy."

We continued on, through trees and along rubble-strewn trails.

"I haven't thanked you for saving me from the Chuma."

Rad stopped and stared at me, his gray eyes looking more like Aladar's now.

"Well?" he said.

"Well, what?"

"Are you going to thank me?"

"I just did."

He shook his head. "No, you stated that you hadn't thanked me. Now you can."

"Are you always like this?" I took a deep breath. "Thank you, Rad, for saving me from the clutches of the dreaded Chuma."

"Think nothing of it, simply happened to be passing by."

He smiled, turned and I ran to catch up as he entered the now empty room with the long table and chairs. My knapsack was also empty, its contents strewn across the table.

"You didn't have to display everything I own." I quickly stuffed my underwear into the bag.

"I didn't. Are all your belongings there?"

"Looks like it. No wait, my journal is missing."

"Your journal?"

"A book I write stuff in. Why would anyone want that?"

"I'm not sure." Rad tapped his finger on his lips. "Is it of any value?"

"To me. It had my poems, mostly personal stuff. Other than

Paul, who else could even read it?" I pushed my jacket on top of everything else and zipped up the knapsack.

"I'll see if anyone knows about this missing journal." He stepped through the door and into the bright sun, his boots crunching over the rubble as he made his way down the street.

Who would've taken it? I closed my eyes, trying to remember what, other than my poems, was in the darn thing. After meeting with Enrial, the leader of the Nereen who had appeared back in my own time, I'd written down everything she'd told me. Anything else? I slapped my forehead. The archive. Afraid I might forget, I'd drawn a map, but not a very good one. Could anyone follow my directions? Even if they did, could they get into the archive without the charm? But what if they did have the charm? Footsteps sounded from outside, fast as though someone were running. Rad jumped through the empty window frame, picked up my knapsack and tossed it to me.

"We'd better get going," he said.

"What about my journal?"

"It's left town by the looks of it." He kicked at one of the chairs, sending it across the room. "Well, are you coming? You do want to get to Holo, don't you?"

"You're taking me?"

"It looks like I'm your only option; Paul appears to have unleashed Arax and the two of them have disappeared."

# Chapter Five

$S$tala rode between Rad and me, legs swaying with her horse's gentle gait and holding her head high on a neck that seemed too slender and proud. I leaned forward and patted my horse under its feathery mane. Its dark coat soaked up the morning sunshine, but the horse seemed untroubled by the heat and continued plodding beside the others.

The only explanation Rad had given for Stala accompanying us was that she'd be needed. For what, I didn't know, but it wasn't for her good nature.

"He was always listening behind corners." She blew air between her lips, sounding much like the horse she rode. "I told you he couldn't be trusted."

"You've been proven right yet again, Stala," Rad said.

They sounded like an old, married couple though she couldn't have been more than twenty-years and he...how old was Rad? Even though he had the same silver-white hair as Aladar, he gave the impression of being much younger.

"When I get my hands on that bat dung, he'll wish he never came to Aten," she said.

"Oh, stop, please." I looked away from them. "I hate when people argue."

"Yes, Stala, do stop." Rad laughed and flicked a bothersome fly from the sleeve of his black coat. "Jodi is much too young to listen to your grumbling."

"I'm not so young," I protested.

"Old beyond your seasons, are you?" he asked.

"I guess you could say that, especially when you consider I come from a time long ago; a time when people were educated, if you know what that means." I clutched the reins, hating the words the minute they rushed out.

Rad pulled his horse to a stop and stared at me. Not anger, not resentment; a look that left me feeling like the fly he'd just evicted.

"You'd be wise to stop boasting where anyone might hear you." He scanned the sand-capped land around us before letting his gaze rest on me. "Educated people, as you so eloquently put it, are a rare commodity around here, quite valuable in fact."

I lowered my head, staring at the spot between my horse's ears. Ever since I'd met Rad, I seemed to always say the wrong thing.

"Why are you coming to Holo with me?" I asked.

"Paul has security details of our city and he's proven himself untrustworthy. We can't have him running loose with that information, can we?" Rad said. "Once I find Paul and drop you in Holo, I'll head home."

He pressed his boots against the horse. "Let's get moving; I'd like to get closer to the Phosphor Caves before nightfall."

The sun dipped low in the sky, its warmth lost and, though my jacket was zipped up, goose bumps coursed up and down my arms.

"How much farther?" I washed down the hard bread I'd eaten with water from one of the plastic bottles Rad had packed. The label was long gone, but I imagined it had once held some grape sport drink.

"I think we'd best call it a day." Rad swung down from the horse, his dusty, black coat rippling after him.

"I'll take first watch," Stala said.

"Fine by me." Rad laid out his animal skin bedding and plopped down on top of it.

After pulling out my flashlight, I set my knapsack on top of the soft bedding I'd been given. Bulging and hard, the knapsack wasn't the greatest pillow, but it would be safe under my head. I glanced around the gray dunes. Would I be safe?

"Why did you come to Aten?" Rad lay on his side, his head propped in his hand.

"Lots of reasons—too many reasons." I leaned back on the knapsack and stared at the sky. "My friend is still here, but I don't even know where. The necklace, the archive, Caden, everything. And now, all that stuff is even more out of my reach than it was before I came back."

I sighed. Stars peeked out overhead and the darkness cushioned me. "I was told by Enrial that I had to return. I'm not exactly sure if she rules the place where the Nera come from or what. I have so many questions and it doesn't look like I'll ever find the answers and, to tell you the truth, I don't know where to start."

"You have to decide what's important to you," Rad said.

"I got the feeling from Enrial that it didn't matter what was important to me. What mattered was Aten and that I could make a difference here."

"Why do you think you can make a difference?" Stala asked. "It's our world, not yours."

"You're wrong, this is my world too," I said. "And I don't know what I'm supposed to do, that's what I'm here to find out. Maybe it's just that I have the key to the archive."

"But you've already lost your necklace. It looks like someone else is going to make the difference," Stala said.

I frowned. No matter what I said, Stala would disagree with me. I didn't want to tell them that Enrial had hinted I had a special ability. They'd never believe it because, as far as I knew, only the Nera's children were born with unusual talents.

"Is Nashira your mother, Rad?" I asked.

He nodded. "It's been some time since I've seen her."

"Then Caden is your half-brother," I said.

He was silent for a moment before answering, "I was unaware of that."

"If she's your mother then you must have a special ability like Caden and Aladar. What's yours?"

An owl hooted in the distance. A perfectly ordinary night sound, yet it made the silence all the more obvious. Stala was building a fire with the kindling we'd brought and she stopped, her hand hovering over the small pile.

"Not one I'm willing to use. Let's get some rest." He lay back and wrapped the animal skin around him.

\* \* \* \*

A loud moan pierced my dreams. I sat up, fumbling for the flashlight, but once I'd found it, was afraid to turn it on.

"Rad? Stala?" I squinted. The fire had died, but I could make out a muddy outline a few meters away.

"I'm here." Stala rose from where she sat beside Rad and came toward me. "It's only Rad's dreams that have awakened you."

"Sounded more like a nightmare." I turned on the flashlight.

"Dreams, nightmares." Stala flipped her hand like a pancake. "Does it matter? Most nights his sleep is burdened by what he cannot leave behind."

Her voice was soft. When I shone the light in her face, she flinched and I turned it off, but not before I'd seen the sadness in her eyes.

"What do you mean?"

"Rad blames himself for too much. He believes he's responsible for what happened."

"Is it something to do with Aladar?"

"No, Aladar never blamed him." Her tone became brisk. "Go back to sleep."

I rested my head against my knapsack and examined the star-studded sky. I'd returned to Aten hoping to find answers. Instead, I'd been confronted by more questions. What memories haunted Rad's dreams? And if Stala wouldn't tell me, how was I going to find out? I stared into the blackness to where Rad slept, quietly now. More questions—why, every time Rad touched me, did it feel as though I'd stuck my finger in an electrical socket? And what was his special ability and why wasn't he willing to use it?

*    *    *    *

A horse whinnied and voices murmured. The early morning air still whispered with the chill of night and I hated the thought of emerging from the warmth of my bedding. I listened to the voices.

"Don't come into the caves with us, Stala."

"You'd never make it through on your own. I'll take you as far as I can, after that, you should be able to manage."

"How long before…"

"I don't know, I've never tried going back. Don't worry, I'll get out before it happens."

Facing away from them, I waited to hear more.

"Not nice to listen in to other's conversations." Rad stood over me. "It's time to go."

"What was I supposed to do, close my ears?" I sat up and wrapped the cover around me. "Why can't Stala stay in the caves?"

"Let's hope you never find out," he said. "We're leaving, eat while you ride."

Why did everyone have to be so mysterious? Even simple questions raised walls. I folded up my covers and tried, awkwardly, to tie them to the horse. Shaking his head, Rad came over and refolded them into a tidy bundle. He had a way a making me feel like a little kid.

"Why are we going into these Phosphor Caves?" I asked.

"Going through the canyon or around would take too long—the quickest route to Holo is underground."

"I hope the caves are safer than the canyon." Neil and I had traveled through Deakin Canyon with Caden's tribe and I'd been caught in a flash flood. It was an experience I didn't want to go through again.

"For you, nowhere on Aten is safe," Rad said. "Or haven't you noticed that?"

It was a challenge getting back on a horse after yesterday's long ride. Like Aladar's tribe, the Awes, we rode without saddles. The ride was a quiet one, but when two jackrabbits sprang from behind a spine-covered bush and zipped across our path, Stala pointed and laughed. She looked different with a smile on her face.

\* \* \* \*

Within an hour, the sun beat a drum on my head. Just as I was about to pull my cap from the knapsack, we rode over a dune and Rad held up his hand. Five boulders, each the size of a dump truck, crowded together on the sand. Water sprang from a deep crevice in one of them and pooled around its base.

"This is it?" He glanced at Stala. "You're sure you want to do this?"

She nodded, all remnants of her smile gone.

"What about the horses?" I asked.

"They stay here for now. Take what you can carry." Rad slid to the ground. "This is when your latest design sack comes in handy."

Rad and Stala used cloth strips to bind supplies onto their backs. Rad carefully rearranged the few things Stala carried and when he was done, he placed his hand on her arm. They stood, staring at one another for a few moments and I looked away.

"Let's go," Rad said.

I stroked my horse's neck and whispered goodbye. Now on foot, I hoped the way through the caves was indeed a shortcut. Stala climbed up one of the boulders, using indentations in the rock I hadn't noticed. Rad waved me forward.

"After you."

Taking a deep breath, I gripped the first tiny notch and pulled myself up. I scraped my foot over the surface, scrambling to find a home and felt Rad steer the bottom of my running shoe into place. Apparently, the strange shock didn't travel through rubber. Several more notches and I threw myself over the top where Stala grabbed my arm and hauled me up. We teetered on the uneven surface, not so high up, but I had the uneasy feeling I would drop off the edge any moment. Rad joined us and I felt better having him between me and a nasty fall. He turned and stared over the Drylands, the toes of his boots hanging over the edge.

"Be careful." Instinctively, I clutched his arm and the tingling, electrical sensation worked its way through his coat to my fingers. "Why is that happening?"

"I assumed it happened with everyone you touched," he said.

"It's there." Stala pointed to a manhole-sized cavity in the boulder. "It's a long way down and slippery. There's a rope hooked into the wall but it's probably not in the best condition."

"You've been here before," I said.

"I was born here."

"In a cave?"

"It was home for most of my life. I never thought I'd come back." Her voice sounded small, like a little kid's.

"I'll go first, then Jodi. Stala, you come when you're ready."

I watched Rad wedge through the hole then disappear into the black shaft. As I bent and grasped the damp rope, Stala stood over me, kneading her knuckles against her thighs.

"Are you going to be okay?" What was so horrible about this place?

She nodded her head. "Let's get it over with."

I pressed my feet and knapsack against the sides and worked my way into the cramped space. With one last look up, I saw Stala reach down to grab the rope. Rad's progress below me was marked with the scratching of his boots against the rock. The light from above dimmed and an impenetrable darkness surrounded me. The grunts and scraping noises coming from below and above were the only evidence that I was not alone.

# Chapter Six

"Almost there." Rad's voice echoed from below.

The shaft ended and my feet burst through. It was only about a two-meter drop, but it would've been nice if Rad had given me a bit more warning. I rolled out of the way to make room for Stala then thrust my hand into my knapsack for the flashlight. Flicking it on, I passed the beam over a small cavern. The rock walls perspired; rivulets of water twisted over bumps and through crevices, eventually making their way under the ground. On the walls, moss sprouted like a boy's first beard, patchy and sparse. Surprisingly, the air was moist and warm. I gave the dimming flashlight to Stala, thankful I'd packed two extra batteries.

"The countdown begins," Stala said. "This way, hurry."

We slipped through a wide fissure in the far wall and continued along a pebbly path. On and on, down and down. The world above ceased to exist; it was only the towering rocks and the three of us. My clothes formed a sweaty coating over my skin, smothering and eating me alive while my mind drifted to a cooler place. Lost in thoughts of snow-covered hills, I bumped into Stala when she stopped and turned to me.

"There's a room ahead where the path narrows, so grab hold of me. I have to turn off the lamp."

With a flick of the switch, the tunnel plummeted into darkness except for a strange, green light radiating from the mossy walls. Grabbing hold of Stala, I lurched after her and could feel a slight pull on my knapsack where Rad must have been holding onto me. A warm breeze brushed my face and an intermittent chirping filled the air. What kind of bird could live without the aid of light? Stala turned to us and I stepped back, gasping. Her eyes were pinpoints of red; two miniscule stoplights close to my face.

"What is it?" she asked.

"Your eyes. I never noticed before."

"Leave, Stala," Rad said.

"I'll take you through this cavern first because there's so many passages, it would be too easy for you to get lost." She turned and the red pinpricks disappeared.

The darkness scared me. The weird chirping sounds scared me. Even the creepy, green walls scared me. But none of those things set my heart thumping like Stala's red eyes. She didn't have those last night. No, something was happening to her down here and if it was happening to her, could it happen to us?

We crept along and the bird sounds got louder, surrounding us. So did an overpowering smell, like a kitty litter that had never been cleaned. The fumes burned my eyes and I staggered back, reached out and leaned against the rock.

"Geez, what's this stuff on the walls?" I wiped my hands on my jeans.

"Bat guano." Rad chuckled.

Of course. Caves and bats. Was there any truth about them sucking blood?

"Keep to this side," Stala said.

Stones loosened by our feet, slid and dropped into the unseen water below. I could almost feel the drop beside me and I pressed against the wall, bat guano or no bat guano. The further along the path we went, the louder the chirping became. A couple of the bats took off from their roosts, then a couple more and, within seconds, the place came alive with the flapping of their wings. I jumped back and raised my hands over my head, imagining their little bat claws clinging to my hair. The ground slithered out from under me and my sneakers skated down the slope. Unfortunately, I was still in them.

Stones splashed below as I sped along the pebble slide, clutching at the passing rocks. When at last the icy water engulfed my legs, I dug in my heels and slithered to a halt. My body trembled like the aftershocks of an earthquake. I no longer cared if my world came to an end in some far-flung future—I wanted to go home, home to my bedroom, home to stupid television shows.

Stones tumbled down the slope, settling beside me as the reassuring surge of Rad's hand on my shoulder banished my homesick thoughts.

"By the nut, Jodi, I'd have given a chief's treasure to have seen you go down that embankment." Rad sounded so much like Aladar in the dark. "We could all use some levity right now."

"Yeah, you should see the comedy routine I've got planned for my big night in Holo."

Rad wrapped his arm around my back, the tingling sensation no longer surprising, no longer frightening, no longer something to be avoided. I clamped my mind shut, afraid of what that might mean.

"There's a rope," he said. "Have you got it? Good, let Stala pull you up."

She must've been much stronger than she looked because she yanked first me then Rad up the slope with no problem. There were lots of things I'd have liked to find out about Stala.

"I'm so sorry," I said, turning my head toward the two red dots hovering near my shoulder. "I've delayed you even longer."

Stala flicked on the flashlight and shone the beam along her arm. Rad and I stepped back—her skin had turned milky-white, the veins glaring through the surface.

"Get out of here," Rad said.

"Leave through the seventh passage, it slopes up. Don't veer off that track and, please, be as quiet as possible." She turned off the flashlight and handed it to me. "I'll take the horses and travel through the canyon."

The red dots blinked then disappeared as she slid around us and traveled back the way we'd come. As soon as we were out of this place, I was going to get some answers.

"Just you and me," Rad said. "Are you ready?"

"Can we turn on the light?" I asked.

"Afraid not. Can't take the chance of attracting too much attention."

Rad led the way along the widening path, counting each opening as it appeared. I slipped on what must have been even more bat guano and Rad grabbed my arm.

"Thanks," I said.

"Where was I?" Rad asked. "Five or six?"

"Five, I think."

The chirping dwindled and soon disappeared completely. By the time we reached the seventh opening, the chill of the water had long passed and I was once again a hot, sweaty, guano-covered mess. Was Stala already heading toward Deakin Canyon, a cool breeze spiking her hair even more? Once above ground, would her eyes and skin return to normal?

Rad turned into the opening and I followed him through. How long had we been in the caves and, more importantly, how long before we got out? A sudden murmur of voices wound through the passage—either the humidity turned my brain to sponge or the bats had learned how to speak. Rad gripped my hand.

"Stay on the track, no matter what," he whispered.

"What are you going to do?"

"Stay with you if I can." He tugged on my hand and we moved forward.

The voices swirled around us, first in front then behind. Everything was dark, the only light coming from the garish green walls. We passed two more openings before entering a torch-lit cavern full of the oddest people I'd ever seen. My breath got tangled in my throat.

They looked like they'd been molded from raw egg whites. The only thing visible within their human shapes were their veins, but they must've had bones or else how could they have started running toward us?

"I think we've taken a wrong turn," Rad said.

We stumbled back through the opening and into the passage, scattering pebbles behind us. Rad pulled me through the first opening we came to. The ground sloped down and we ran back out, ducked into the next opening and followed a tunnel that seemed to lead up. Up toward the surface. Up out of here. Voices boomed behind us. Rad stopped and threw me ahead.

"Go!"

"What about you?"

"Get out of here. Find Aladar." He glanced over his shoulder. "Now!"

I walked backward until I could no longer see him by the green light of the moss, then turned and ran up the path, sobs spilling out instead of breaths. I ran until my heart threatened to explode right out of my chest. Then I fell to my knees.

I couldn't leave him there, not with those jelly people. I unzipped the side pocket of my knapsack and seized the knife. It felt small in my hand, but it might give me just enough of an edge to help Rad. I left the knapsack and raced back down the path, trying to ignore the terror that was swallowing me whole.

# Chapter Seven

I held the knife in front of me. Gramps' knife that had, up till now, only sharpened twigs and cut fishing line on our camping trips. If he were here, he'd take it gently away and tell me I shouldn't play with sharp objects. Oh, Gramps, if only you were here!

The clatter of voices in the tunnel had ceased and I crept close to the wall, slashing the tiny blade in the air as I turned each dark corner. I couldn't have run that far, so where was Rad? Where were the jelly people?

I splashed through a puddle; a puddle that hadn't been there when I'd raced up the path earlier. Where had I gone wrong? The green walls cast an almost candlelight glow in the tunnel, not revealing the path far ahead, but shedding enough light to make me aware of every shadow. Standing still, I angled my head to the side and heard a sucking noise to my right. I bounced away, brandishing my weapon.

"Stay back!" My voice quivered.

The sound advanced. The knife trembled in my fingers and, afraid I might drop it, I wrapped both hands around the slippery handle.

"Why don't you put that down?" A slurpy voice said. "You could hurt someone."

A shadow separated from the wall and glided toward me. I opened my mouth to scream, but a wisp of air was the only thing that made its way up my throat.

"Never seen the likes of me, huh?" His eyes glowed a bright red.

"What...where is my friend?"

"Questions." He batted his jellyfish arm back and forth. "I do like stories, but what makes you think I like questions?"

He had no clothes on which seemed all right because he had no skin either—just veins and eyeballs. I kept my gaze on the red pinpoints and, when he spoke, the jelly on what must have been his face, rippled. He circled around me.

"Truth is, I haven't seen many the likes of you either." He stopped in front of me. "How can you stand being stitched up in that casing? How do you move? Don't you just itch to get out?"

He reached out to touch me and I drew back. For someone who didn't like questions, he sure asked a lot of them.

"Where's my friend?" I asked again. I strained my eyes as I looked for an escape.

"Come with me." He flowed along the path, reminding me of encyclopedia pictures that showed the inside of a human body. It was gross on paper, yet in reality, it was like watching a jellyfish ballet. I wanted to run, but wanted to find Rad more.

"You've made the right decision coming into our caves. Much too dry Upworld, isn't it? I've never been, but the horror stories." His skinless shoulders shuddered. "Once you and your friend are finished, you must tell me all about your life there."

"Once I'm finished what?" But I had a horrible feeling I already knew the answer. I backed away from him and smacked into something. Whipping around, I came face-to-face with another of his kind. This one held a spear, its tip a jagged piece of crystal.

"Keep moving." He prodded me with it.

I inched along the path, sorry that I'd not listened to Rad. Nearing the end, a jelly woman stepped forward. Without skin, it wasn't that easy to tell the difference, but this one had a head full of blond hair reaching far down her back. She cranked open a metal gate that badly needed oiling, and pushed me inside. The gate clanged shut behind me.

"Enjoy the transformation," called my guide. "Oh, and do come and tell your stories when you emerge."

"What are you doing here?" Rad veered around a black pool of water in the middle of the floor and glared at me. A torch burned brightly on the wall.

"I couldn't leave you here."

"You should've kept running. You're supposed to make it to Holo." He shook his head. "This isn't what's meant to happen."

"How could you know what's meant to happen?" I glanced over my shoulder and lowered my voice. "Are these jelly people going to hurt us?"

"They're called Kurage and, as far as they're concerned, they hope to help us."

"Please stop treating me like I haven't a brain in my head; like everything is a mystery that simple-minded, little Jodi couldn't possibly understand." Exasperated, I threw my knife against the wall and folded my arms across my chest, hiding my shaking hands.

"Sit down."

"I'll stand, thank you." I tapped my foot on a rock, the sound muffled by the damp moss that grew throughout our little cave.

"You're right, you're not a child, though sometimes you do act like one." He paced beside the water. "These people believe the sun and everything else Upworld, as they call it, is hazardous. And, to them, it is; they can't leave the caves. Stala did, but someone who obviously knew how it could be done helped her transform. You saw what happened to her after we got here."

The eyes, the skin, the veins. Oh, yes, I saw what happened.

"The Kurage will simply hold us here until we too take on their barely perceptible form. I don't know how long it will take before it happens, but it will happen." Rad stopped in front of me. "After that, we'd fry out in the hot sun and dry air."

"Like an egg." I shuddered. "We can escape, there's only a few of them."

"There's more everywhere in these caves. They believe they're doing us a favor; they'd rather kill us quickly down here than let us return to a horrible death Upworld."

"But how does it happen?" I couldn't imagine how it would be possible for our bodies to change so drastically. "Why did Stala change so quickly?"

"It's the spores in this." Rad kicked at the moss-covered ground. "Stala told me it changes all who enter and remain in the caves. She knew it could affect her faster than us; her body must still retain some essence of its basic form."

We were interrupted by the sound of sloshing footsteps coming down the passage.

"Food for them?" The gate creaked open. "Take it in, go on, what are you waiting for?"

I turned away. I didn't want to be reminded of what was to come if we couldn't get out of there.

"Stala?" Rad's voice was filled with horror.

I looked up. Unclothed, yet revealing nothing, a milky form held a green woven tray. Her short, spiky, blond hair looked as though she'd chopped it off in the dark and her eyes, red pinpoints of misery, bobbed up and down. She set down the tray, on top of which a pale, eyeless fish flopped alongside a heaping of gray moss.

"They caught me before I could escape." It was Stala's voice. "It all happened so fast, I thought I'd have more time."

"Stala," Rad repeated. His hands hovered above her shoulders then he clamped them down. "Come with us. We might be able to get away."

"No, I can't go through it again—changing back." She shook her head and her spiky hair wavered in the torchlight.

"You're not supposed to be here," Rad said.

"Be quick in there," the spear holder poked his head into the cavern. "Out you come, Stala."

She ducked from Rad's grasp and slid to the opening. "The pool is very deep, so watch your step because you never know where you'll end up."

The spear-holder ushered her out and she was gone. A landslide of emotions ran through me—disgust, guilt and a crushing heartache. I remembered Stala's smile when she'd seen the jackrabbits, the only smile I'd ever witnessed on her face. Was Rad in love with her? If so, what must he be feeling? Gone was the roguish twinkle, as if someone had turned out the lights. He lowered himself onto a rock and cradled his head in his hands.

"Rad, I'm sorry, I don't know what to say."

"Nothing, say nothing."

If I hadn't told anyone about the necklace, then Paul wouldn't have taken off and Stala would still be digging into the past, a straw hat covering her head. Rad blamed me, of course. I stood by the pool, averting my tear-filled eyes from the flopping fish that was, like me, totally out of its element. The still water reflected none of the torchlight. Deep, she'd said. Yes, I could imagine it went on forever.

"Rad?" I whispered.

He didn't answer.

"Rad, the water." I hesitated before folding my hand around the gasping fish and dropping it into the water where it disappeared into the inky depths. My fingers twitched as I lowered them into the cold pool. "We can get out of here."

"We'll never get out."

Anger burned in my throat and I rushed to him, pushing his shoulders back so he was forced to look at me.

"How can you deny Stala her one chance of saving us? She's given us a lifeline, are you going to throw it back in her face?" I prodded him, making sure he got zapped. "Well, I'm not going to disappoint her and if you were any kind of friend, you wouldn't either."

I stalked to the edge of the pool. "Are you coming?"

Rad's eyes glinted and a smile, the tiniest of smiles, curved the corners of his mouth. He tore off his black coat and pulled a strip of cloth from the makeshift knapsack he'd worn in the tunnels. After he'd gently tied one end around my wrist, he held the other end out to me. I double-knotted it around his wrist—there was no way I'd let him be separated from me.

"Take a deep breath," he said.

We jumped into the cold, black water.

# Chapter Eight

If my jaws hadn't been clamped shut, the icy water would've knocked the breath right out of my chest. Once submerged, we dove down and I stretched out my free hand, feeling the rough rock and praying for an opening. Rad tugged on our cloth binding and we swam forward. I pressed my hand up and hit solid rock; we must've been in an underwater tunnel and my lungs were about to burst. Stala would believe we'd escaped, even if we died down here. But I wanted to live and, with the last of my strength, I kicked my legs. Tiny, bright lights pierced my lids. I had no oxygen left.

Weightless and rising, even the rock ceiling couldn't hold me down. I couldn't hold my breath any longer and opened my mouth, but instead of water, I sucked in air—fresh, wholesome air. Rad pulled me from the pool into a cavern, its wide opening blazing with sunshine. He untied the cloth around my wrist before working on his own, but it must have tightened in the water. I nudged away his hand and stabbed at the knot with my dirty fingernails until, finally, it came loose. Rad straightened out the length of wet cloth then dropped it into the water where it floated for a moment before sinking into the murky pool. We rose and stumbled toward the light and Deakin Canyon, with its multi-colored walls, opened up before us.

"The sun." I spread my arms, soaking up its dry warmth. "I didn't think we'd ever see it again."

"Let's get out of here."

Something in his voice had changed and I peeked at him—the same Rad, though wetter. He must have been thinking of Stala, missing her. It was only right he should grieve; he'd lost someone he cared for and as sad as I was for Stala, I was a little sad for myself, too. On the way down the rocky path, Rad stopped and looked back, his gaze roving over the entrance to the cavern as if memorizing it. After several minutes, we continued on.

"Night's coming," Rad said, "and I'm getting hungry. How about you?"

"Starving." I glanced at my watch. "We were in there most of the day; it seemed longer."

"I'm not much of a fisherman, I'm afraid. Are you any good?"

"Not with my bare hands and there isn't much else down here." The river rushed alongside us, cutting a path through the canyon.

"We'd better get out of here then." He didn't sound very excited at the prospect.

We trudged up the next path leading out of Deakin Canyon, my breath coming fast and furious as we climbed. When we reached the top, I hunched over, my hands on my knees. Staring at my feet, I waited for my breath to return to normal.

"I'm so hungry, I could even eat one of those oozing, blue fruits Aladar once offered me," I said.

"You may get your chance."

I raised my head.

"Take a look." He waved his arm. "We're here."

The same lush, green trees, the same moss growing up the trunks and the same red flowers hanging from twisting vines. Fall had descended on the world around us, but the Awes forest seemed immune to the changing season. The first time I'd been beside the forest, Caden warned it wasn't safe to venture in uninvited.

"Can we go in?"

"It doesn't look like we have much choice," Rad said.

"Will there be any paths or will the trees block our way?" The Awes forest barred any uninvited travelers.

"This used to be my home." With his hand on the small of my back, Rad ushered me under the great canopy.

The trees opened up in front of us, revealing a narrow strip of the moss-laden forest floor. Rad reached up, plucked a hidden fruit from one of the branches and handed it to me.

"Sorry, it's not a jaka," he said.

"I was only kidding, I don't think I'd eat one of those blue things no matter how hungry I was. This looks good." I bit down into the red, pear-shaped fruit and the juice ran down my chin.

Rad reached up again.

"I always wondered how Bix gathered the food," I said. "I see now it was quite simple."

"Old Bix, is he still serving Aladar his meals?"

"How long has it been since you've been home?" I asked.

Rad paused, gazing into the trees. "A long time. I left after my sixteenth, three celebrations ago."

So Rad was only nineteen years old. We continued walking along the path as it opened then pushed closed behind us.

"Where are we headed?"

"The path will figure that out," Rad said.

"Why do you have to make everything so mysterious?"

"You're right, I forgot you're not a child." He grinned. "The path is leading us to where it believes I want to go. I may not know, but it does."

I sighed. "I give up."

As much as Rad didn't seem to want to return to the forest, his spirits had lifted ever since we'd ducked under its branches. Maybe the forest did that to all the Awes. I'd probably feel the same walking through my own neighborhood.

"It's getting dark." I squinted, glimpsing the coming night through the leaves.

"The path will stop at a suitable clearing when we need rest."

"We don't have magical things where I live."

"From what Paul told us, there's been many changes since your time. Now I'm not sure I can believe anything he said."

"I don't think Paul's all bad. He wants to make his mark here and believes having control of the archive will do it." I frowned. "He's weak, not the kind of person to take care of it."

"And just who would be the ideal caretaker of your archive?" Rad asked.

"My friend Neil's dad, Mr. Moran."

Rad stared at me. I don't think he was used to being surprised.

"What is it?" I asked.

"You know Ed Moran?"

"Yes," I stepped toward him, "and it's obvious you do, too. Have you seen him? Have you seen Neil?"

"If you'd stayed in Kopi awhile longer, you'd have seen them."

"Why didn't you tell me?"

"How could I have known? You never mentioned their names. They've been living with us for over seven seasons."

"Seven?" I calculated how many years that was—almost two. "I don't understand, I thought only a couple of months had passed since I'd left. What are they doing in Kopi?"

"Ed built the windmills, for one thing, but they never told us much about themselves and come and go as they please."

I slid down one of the trees, its rough bark biting into my back. I'd been so close to them. "They never told you they knew me?"

Rad shook his head.

"They must've said something about Aladar."

"I don't normally encourage talk about my family," Rad said.

"They're okay? Healthy? Neil, is he happy?"

"They seem to be."

"That's good." My eyes brimmed with tears. "I wasn't sure they'd escaped from the Major."

Rad patted his sides, seeming to look in coat pockets that no longer existed. Finally, he pulled out his shirttail and held it near my face.

"Go ahead, blow."

I couldn't help but laugh. "I'm not going to blow my nose on your shirt."

"It's all right or, as Neil would say, no problem. I'm willing to sacrifice a bit of clothing for a good cause."

"I'm fine. No, I'm more than fine." I swatted his hand away. "It's enough knowing they're safe."

Rad tucked his shirt back in.

"Let's find a better place for the night," he said, motioning me through the trees that opened then closed once we'd passed through.

I couldn't explain how I felt hearing about Neil and his dad—excited, disappointed, happy. It was like I'd won the lottery, but couldn't collect the money for another year.

"This is the spot." Rad looked around a small clearing.

"Looks the same as the one we just left."

"Ah, this one has a good sized sleeping area and an abundance of dried moss. The forest always knows."

I sat down. He was right; dry moss covered almost every surface. If Bix were here, he'd cover me with a blanket and fluff me up a pillow made from the special Awes fabric. Rad ripped a great strip of moss from a nearby tree and laid it over my knees, and after ripping away another piece, he sat down with it on the other side of the clearing.

When I'd first come to Aten, I'd spent a night alone with Caden. I'd been a nervous wreck, yet I didn't feel that way with Rad; I was relaxed, contented as though I were with someone I'd known all my life.

"Are we going to look for Aladar?" I asked.

"I suspect he'll find us."

"How does he do that?"

"The trees tell him," Rad said. "That's his special ability. Now let's get some rest."

I nodded to the growing darkness and lay down. The moss smelled earthy, comforting and I snuggled into it, letting the kitten-soft fibers warm my skin. I closed my eyes and listened to the forest sounds. A familiar chirping echoed from the tree above me.

"Rad?"

"Yes," he mumbled.

"I think there's a bat in the tree."

"It won't hurt you, not in the forest."

The chirping started up again. I stared into gray branches and pulled the thick, moss blanket up to my chin.

"Do you want to come over here?" Rad asked.

"Can I?"

"Come on." He sighed. "I can't believe someone who would jump into a black pool of water not knowing if there's a way out, could be frightened by a little bat."

"You should see me with spiders." I shuffled over to him, lugging my moss blanket behind me. "Thank you, Rad."

"See, saying thank you isn't all that difficult, is it?"

I lay a few meters from him and closed my eyes.

The memory of Stala stabbed at me in the darkness. She remained trapped far below with the bats and the Kurage, and all because of me. I curled my arms over my chest and tried to thrust the unwanted image of her jelly-like body out of my mind. If thoughts of Stala haunted me, then they must be tearing Rad apart. Would he ever forgive me for involving her? Would I ever forgive myself?

The chirping had changed to a hum, a sweeter sound. I opened my eyes. A red flower hung over me, emitting its honey odor while a hummingbird, its compact body a vivid purple, vibrated near the blossom. This was the magic of the forest.

"It's time to get moving."

I propped myself up on my elbow and Rad passed me another of the pear-like fruits, as perfectly ripe as it could be.

"Thanks," I said.

"You'd better watch it, thanking me is becoming somewhat of a habit with you."

"Then you'll have to stop being nice to me." I smiled up at him, but he was staring behind me, his own smile fading. I looked over my shoulder.

"And how, may I ask, could anyone stop being nice to you?" Aladar said.

# Chapter Nine

Aladar's billowing clothes encircled him, catching then drowning the sun and shadows in the shimmering, green fabric. He opened his arms.

"Aladar!" I tossed the fruit behind me as I ran to him.

"We didn't think you were able to return to Aten," Aladar whispered, pressing his cheek against my hair.

"I came back right away, but so much time has passed. I don't know how that's possible, and the Major has Caden, and, Catta—you remember her..." My words were strung together like Christmas lights.

Aladar held up his hand. "Slow down."

I breathed deeply then opened my mouth to speak again.

"I hadn't realized you two knew each other quite so well." Rad slapped invisible particles from his sleeve. "I'll leave you in Aladar's capable hands."

"Leave me?"

"I should continue my search for Paul."

"You don't need to leave, Radala. This is still, and always will be, your home." Aladar's voice was strained.

"Kopi is my home."

I walked over the moss carpet and laid my hand on Rad's arm, the energy surging between us in waves.

"Please don't go, we can search together."

Rad gazed at my hand for a moment, then nodded. "I suppose it would be good to see everyone in Windore."

I turned to Aladar. Deep lines ran between his eyes, but when he spotted me watching, he smiled.

"It's all set then." He snapped his fingers.

That's when I knew that coming back to Aten had been the right thing to do. When I'd first met Aladar, his constant finger snapping drove me around the bend. Now the familiar sound wrapped around me like a cozy blanket.

Three horses waited for us deeper in the forest—not only had the trees told Aladar there were visitors, they must have told him how many. Aladar and I rode side-by-side while Rad forged a few meters ahead. I tried to include him in the conversation, but he seemed content to listen from whatever world he'd escaped to. Aladar knew about Caden's capture, but had, so far, been unable to discover where the Major had imprisoned him. He seemed most interested in Enrial.

"I knew there was a special energy surrounding you."

Rad's head snapped up when Aladar said this.

"The charm on your necklace is useless to the Major," Aladar continued.

"He can use it to get into the archive," I said.

"No, only you can use it and the Major knows that."

"How can you be so sure?"

"He doesn't only want the necklace, he wants you. He's made that clear. Enrial or whoever created the key, would've made sure the archive could only be opened by the one person…" Aladar shifted on his horse.

"What?" I asked.

"Jodi, you exist here for a reason. Someone produced you to perform a duty."

"No one produced me. How can you say that?"

Aladar pulled his horse to a stop. "What do you see, Radala?"

Rad's back straightened. "She goes to Holo. After that, she's lost from my sight."

"What are you two talking about?" But I knew. I put together all the little hints that had surfaced since I'd first met Rad. "You can see the future, that's your special ability."

"It's my curse."

"And after Holo, I don't exist anymore?" My stomach plummeted to a place somewhere around my toes.

"No, it's simply that I can't see wherever it is you go."

"Why didn't you tell me?" I said.

Aladar coughed. "We'll discuss this when we get to Windore."

"Is Windore your home?" I really wanted to ask if I was human or something Enrial had invented; ask if she had tricked me; and I especially wanted to know if I was meant to die before I'd accomplished anything on Aten. But I didn't think either Aladar or Rad had those answers.

"Windore's our forest city. You'll like it there." Aladar snapped his fingers and we rode on.

I would disappear off Rad's radar screen after Holo. What did that mean?

"You're going to tell me everything when we get to Windore," I said.

We didn't speak for the rest of the short trip. The only sounds were the horse's hooves whispering over the forest floor.

Light bounced over the forest city. The houses embroidering a wide street jutted out from the trees almost as though they were part of the thick trunks. The buildings were covered in blue moss and I wanted to touch them to make sure they weren't an illusion. People strolled past, each dressed in the green, weightless Awes fabric. I tried to think of a word, any word, to describe Windore's beauty, but none existed.

"How could you leave this place, Rad?" I asked.

"I'd like to know the answer to that as well," Aladar said. "You like it, Jodi?"

"Oh, Aladar, it's beautiful and haunting."

His eyes gleamed and I knew he was pleased. He turned to Rad. "Welcome home."

Rad's normally somber, gray eyes soaked in the blue of the city. He seemed to be as awestruck as I was.

"I didn't think I'd missed it." He took a deep breath. "I'll enjoy this short visit."

People approached, smiles wide as they greeted Rad and he was pulled away, lost amidst the back patting of the men and embraces of the women. Aladar had once told me the Awes women were beautiful. That had been an understatement; each had fair, almost silver hair curling down her back. Wearing the same pants and tops as the men, the women's slim figures only seemed to be flattered by the Awes fabric. I hunched down on my horse and felt as though I'd left the house in my pajamas. Aladar smirked and opened his mouth.

"Please don't make a joke," I said. "I'm not in the mood."

"Ah, Jodi, I fear your innocence has been lost since I last saw you. I'll miss it."

"You'll miss having me to fall for all your pranks. Can we go somewhere and talk?"

With a nod, he indicated one of the nearby buildings. "We'll talk about old, and new, times over a brew."

I wasn't old enough to drink, but didn't think they had any age limit on Aten. "What about the horses?"

"Leave them, they'll find their way back to the stables."

There was no door to the building and we entered through a large arch. Inside, smooth wooden benches and tables circled the largest oak tree I'd ever seen—it would easily take ten people to wrap their arms around its trunk. I bent back my neck and saw that the tree grew straight through a hole in the ceiling. After sitting, we were served two steaming cups of dark liquid.

Testing the drink on my lips, I said, "It's like tea."

"Is that not the taste you were expecting?"

I shrugged. "I'm so tired of being the only person who doesn't seem to know what's going on. Can I ask my questions now?"

"Ask away."

"Exactly how long have I been gone?"

"Nine seasons."

Over two years. "How did you get away from the Major's soldiers at the archive?"

"Remember that box Ed Moran took before we re-entered the elevator?"

"The emergency kit," I said.

"After the Major took you back toward the archive, Ed set off a flare that was contained in the box." Aladar smiled. "Scared the limbs right off the soldiers, they ran every which way. By the time we got inside, you were gone and the Major had pulled his disappearing act."

"I think it's the brooch," I tapped my chest, "he wears here. That must be where he gets his power. And I have a feeling the brooch calls to me. I've given this a lot of thought and, as much as I hate to admit it, I always feel drawn to the Major. Like he has something I need."

"What could you need from that lump of a man?" Aladar wrinkled his nose. "When did you feel this?"

"When Nashira helped me escape through the tunnels under Holo and, during the battle, I'm sure the Major was on the other side of the barrier; I could feel him. And when we met him in the Drylands, it was only because Neil stopped me that I didn't reveal myself to the Major." I took a sip of the cooling tea. "Can you imagine being attracted to that guy?"

"He must have some kind of power over you and, so far, you've not fallen victim to it. You'll have to be careful."

"The Major seems to have everyone on Aten hunting me. How did he know I'd return?"

"He obviously knows more about the power of the necklace than even you do."

I nodded. The Major had known that the snake charm could open the archive, so he must've known it would allow me to travel between times. Did it have any other powers? People walked past the arch, arms linked, chatting and laughing.

"Why does Rad call his ability a curse?"

"That's not my answer to give. Any more questions?"

I leaned back, pretending I didn't care, but I did care, more than I wanted to admit. "Why didn't Neil and Mr. Moran stay with you?"

"They wanted to travel and uncover the secrets of Aten. I've seen them on several occasions, once in Nereen." He smiled when he noticed the look of surprise on my face. "Oh, yes, until recently, Nashira had opened the doors of Nereen to men. Of course, with all that's been happening lately, she's closed them once again. I saw Neil and his father again near the archive. I believe they go there, hoping to find a way in without the key."

"How're Nashira and the rest of the Nera?"

"Much has changed since you left." He frowned. "The Major somehow contrived to shut down the outports and the Nera are, for all intents and purposes, stranded in Nereen."

Traveling in the Nera's outports was like being squeezed through the eye of a needle, but they were speedy and safe and you could get across vast distances in seconds. Even though they were now too old to have any more children, the Nera were often the target of kidnappers. That was why they needed the outports. Nereen may have had more amenities than the rest of Aten, but I couldn't imagine the women would be happy to hide there for the rest of their lives.

"I'll go there after I find the necklace and Caden." I bit my lip, dreading the answer to my next question. "Is Caden really married to Catta?"

"He wasn't when I last saw him, not so long ago, but you've got to remember that you've been gone for some time. The Major obviously believed you'd return, but no one else did. I suspect the Major already knows you're here and will double his efforts to find you. If you insist on following Catta, then getting into Holo unnoticed will prove a challenge."

"What do you think Rad meant when he said I'm lost from sight after Holo?"

"Radala's ability can be selective."

"I never knew his real name was Radala." I pressed my palms on the smooth wooden tabletop. "You two look so much alike."

Aladar had always fascinated me and I believed he used his arrogance to hide a soft underbelly. It was after the battle in Nereen that I'd realized how important he was to me. Exhausted from the fighting, he'd slung his arm over my shoulder—not only giving comfort but seeming to take some from the contact as well. Aladar had gone from being my captor to being one of the few people I could rely upon on Aten. I gazed at him now and chuckled as the realization hit me. Yes, he was arrogant, but he was magical and strong, too.

"I missed you," I said.

He smiled. "You sound surprised."

"I am, considering that you used your ability to tie up Caden with your vines then kidnap me. Most people may not see the real you, but I do."

"We'll keep that secret between the two of us." Aladar winked, but was unable to hide the blush that spread over his cheeks. "As far as Radala's vision is concerned, it could mean you're to return to your own time after you're finished in Holo."

"I don't want to go back. Aten is my time now."

"Perhaps, by then, you'll have accomplished what Enrial sent you here to do."

"She doesn't control me."

"You may have no choice."

"I'll still be around after Holo, no matter what Rad does or doesn't see." I stood, walked to the arch and gazed at the beautiful city beyond. Turning back, I smiled. "I don't know what I'd do without you, Aladar."

I stepped into a passing crowd and was swept down the street. I needed cheering and I knew just the person who could help me.

# Chapter Ten

Windore was a fairy tale kingdom—hazy and soft around the edges, it was as though I was viewing it through a dream. Awes smiled and nodded, their whispers following me as I passed. Was it my curly, auburn hair, my unusual clothing, or the fact that I'd arrived with Rad that drew their interest?

I strolled along the wide, moss-covered street, my steps kicking up the sharp scent of thyme. Mats, woven from thick vines, lay scattered under the long branches of an ancient-looking maple tree. Bolts of fabric, bows and arrows, and finely crafted jewelry adorned the mats. The bracelets, rings and necklaces winked at me.

"Would you like to try something on?" A woman beckoned to me.

"I haven't any money."

"Money?"

"Anything to trade," I said.

"Let's not worry about that." She picked up a silver bracelet and held it out to me.

I shook my head and bent over the necklaces. "That one, with the snake charm. Where did you get it?"

"A friend described the design to me and I thought I'd try my hand at it. I made two of them. Do you like it?"

"May I try it on?"

She slipped the chain over my head and the charm settled on my chest. Almost identical to my own necklace, the imitation lacked only the reassuring coolness.

"Where do you get your silver," I asked.

"The forest holds many riches. You can keep it." She pointed to the necklace. "I was going to melt it down anyway, no one else has shown any interest."

"Who has the other one?"

"My friend, Bix." She narrowed her eyes. "Am I right in thinking it was your own necklace he described?"

I nodded. "Where can I find him?"

"After all the patrols he's been on lately, I imagine he's in the meditation gardens, resting in the sun." She pointed down the street. "I'm sure you'll find him there."

After thanking her, I strode toward an area where the rambling noise of Windore's streets was muffled. Here, children dashed and giggled, their laughter like chimes in a summer breeze. Narrow paths wrapped around trees, and blossoms the size of baseball gloves grew from bushes and plants in the most unearthly colors—purples and yellows, but not quite like any colors I'd seen before. Small, sparrow-like birds dashed between the plants. So intrigued by it all, I was startled when I turned around and found a horde of kids following me.

"Hello," I said.

"Are you her?" One little boy stepped forward, his curly, white hair scraping his shoulders.

"Am I who?"

"The girl from outside?"

"I suppose I am. Why do you ask?"

They huddled together, whispering.

"Bix said he was going to marry you," said the boy as he drew his head away from the others.

"He did, did he? Have you seen him?"

Without another word, the boy took my hand and led me along a path, letting go only when we reached a small clearing. A stream spilled water into a rocky pool and filled the small space with a refreshing mist. Bix, lounging on a bench and eating from a tray of fruit, sprang up when he saw me, sending the fruit tumbling onto the bench and into the water. The kids found this uproariously funny.

"Jodi!" Bix waved his hands. "Off with the rest of you, off you go."

"Howdy, Bix."

"I never, no I never thought…well, this is wonderful, can't tell you…"

"It's good to see you, too." I glanced over my shoulder, making sure all the kids had gone. "What's this I hear about you and me getting married?"

"What did those children say?" His cheeks glowed. "Don't listen to them, always making up stories."

Bix cleared the fruit from the bench, sat and patted the space beside him. Resting, I told him everything that had happened since I'd last seen him. Saying it out loud helped to get it all sorted in my head.

"It's been at least five days since I saw Catta. She must be in Holo by now and if she's given the necklace to the Major, then…" I closed my eyes and leaned back. "I can't see how I'll ever get it back from him."

"Aladar believes only you can open the archive."

"That's even scarier because it means the Major will keep looking for me."

"You could stay here." He turned away. "You could stay with me."

"Oh, Bix." Tears crept into the corners of my eyes. "I can't stay here or anywhere else that's safe. I have to go to Holo and, as scary as it is, I might have to meet up with the Major."

He spread his sausage-like fingers over his knees.

"Then you'll need to get ready for the trip. Come on, we've a lot of work to do."

Bix hovered behind me, his hands clasping and unclasping. "What do you think?" he asked.

I stared into the polished metal surface at my reflection. Gone were the red hair, watch and jeans and, in their place, a tangle of silver-white curls and the soft Awes clothing.

"I don't know what to think." I leaned forward. "I don't even recognize myself."

"That's the idea. Now you can enter Holo without the guards dragging you back into the dungeons."

I nodded. If I were unlucky enough to end up in the underground dungeons of Holo again, there would be no Nashira to help me escape.

"Let's see if we can fool Aladar," Bix said.

Aladar greeted us at the door and his eyes widened when he saw my transformation. He circled around me. "It's astounding. You fought me before about acting like an Awes, but now your metamorphosis is almost complete. Come in."

I'd expected Aladar to live in Windore's largest house, yet when I'd met him patrolling his forest, he seemed quite happy with only trees for shelter and a fire for warmth. His small room held a hammock for a bed and four hammock chairs grouped around a polished tree stump. The night had grown cool and a fire glowed beside Rad as he lazed in a chair, an arm resting on his upraised knee. He stared, dragging his gaze over me.

I shrugged, hating the heat that crept into my cheeks. "How else can I get into Holo?"

"Yes, getting into Holo." Aladar snapped his fingers. "We were just talking about that. Would you like to tell her our plan, Radala?"

Later, alone in my own room and lying in the hammock I'd been given for the night, I went over their so-called plan. Aladar would travel through Deakin Canyon toward Ganodu and, hopefully, meet up with Catta. He'd drawn a map to the archive and given it to his brother, saying, "You may need this if your own plans don't work out."

Aladar had convinced Rad to give up his search for Paul in order to accompany me to Holo. That's where the plan became a bit fuzzy because there was no way of knowing what would happen there. Bix had suggested it would be best if I didn't go into Holo at all, but Rad had shaken his head.

"No, she's meant to go," he'd said.

Could we find Caden, never mind free him? I didn't even know if he was in Holo. And if Catta had delivered the necklace, I doubted the Major would return it to me.

I turned on my side, sending the narrow hammock rocking. I hadn't allowed myself to think about Caden these last few days, but now tried to visualize him in my mind—his copper-colored skin; long, dark hair; and eyes that could drill straight into my soul. I'd loved him so much. I sat up and swung my legs over the side of the hammock. Why was I thinking in the past tense? He was still alive and I loved him and would do everything I could to free him from the Major. I lay down, imagining Caden's arms around me, and my eyelids drifted closed. It wasn't until morning that I remembered the phantom tingling sensation that had accompanied me into slumber land.

"How long will it take us to get there?" I tried to settle comfortably amidst the bundles of food Bix had layered over my horse.

"You'll be there by day's end," Bix said. "Always best to pack as much as you can."

"We'll meet back here." Aladar's hand rested on the neck of Rad's horse. "Be careful, both of you."

We rode along the empty path toward the forest and, glancing back, I saw Aladar watching us. We turned a bend and he was lost from sight.

"How did you enjoy your visit home?" I asked.

Rad smiled. *"Mid pleasure and palaces though we may roam, be it ever so humble, there's no place like home."*

I pulled on the reins and stared at him. "I forget who wrote it, but that's a famous quote. How do you know it?"

"By John Howard Payne and if I tell you, you'll have to admit you were wrong that Paul was the only one in Kopi capable of reading and writing."

"No paper or books could've survived."

"Not paper, not books—plaques, magnets, cups. It's amazing what you people felt compelled to put your words upon."

"And that's how you learned to read?" My horse stopped for a moment when a chipmunk zigzagged across our path, a golf-ball sized nut clenched in its mouth.

"With help from Paul," Rad said.

"If he wanted to make an important contribution to Aten, he should've been happy just teaching you to read."

We rode in easy silence, stopping only once to eat. A bird chirped from its hidden perch and, if I closed my eyes, I could imagine this was my own forest back home. The first time I'd come through here, I'd been Aladar's prisoner and had actually looked forward to arriving in Holo. This time, I wanted the lush canopy to shelter me forever.

\* \* \* \*

We emerged from the forest late in the day. Holo lay far below us inside its dusty crater. Nothing seemed to have changed—four long roads led down to low, brown buildings and the same spike-filled ditch encircled the market town. I slid from my horse, then stroked its soft nose with trembling fingers.

"We'll stay in the forest tonight," Rad said, "and lose ourselves amongst the merchants traveling into Holo tomorrow."

"This is it, then." I tried to laugh. "This is where I've wanted to come for the past week, and now that I'm here, all I want to do is run away."

Rad, having changed into Awes clothing, looked more like Aladar than ever before.

"Perhaps I can ease your mind." He steered me back into the forest. Holding my hand,he raised his gaze to mine. "I've learned to ignore most everything I see of the future, but there's never been such complete darkness before. I don't believe you disappear from sight after Holo, I do."

"What does that mean?" My fingers curled tightly around his, the tingling current seeming to fuse us together.

"I always thought I'd welcome the end of living with this curse," Rad said. "Now, I think I'd like to hang on awhile longer."

"I don't want you to come with me to Holo."

"There's nothing I can do about that. You see, I'm meant to go to Holo with you."

I stared around at the forest, hoping an answer would pop out from behind a tree. "Just because it's what you've seen, doesn't mean it has to be. We have control over our own destinies."

Rad shook his head. "Whatever I see, does happen and there's nothing I can do to change that. It's always been that way."

I got up and paced in front of him. "I won't be able to live with myself knowing I was responsible for..." I couldn't even say the words. "I won't let it happen."

"If anyone could do it, I'm sure it would be you." Rad smiled. "We'll celebrate tonight."

"What is there to celebrate?"

"Friendship." Rad got up and pulled the bundles from our horses.

# Chapter Eleven

The wagons and carts clattered along the sun-soaked road and sent up a swirl of dust. I remembered the cowl neck of the Awes' clothes and pulled it over my nose and mouth. I felt as if I was going back to a time long ago, but in my reality, I'd been here only two weeks before.

Each step the horses took drew us closer to the guards with their tin-pot hats and I hoped none of them were like Murdy, the abusive guard Caden had killed. My breath was shallow, and I could hardly hold onto the reins with my shaking fingers.

"Try and relax, they've a nose for fear," Rad whispered.

"Then I'll be smelling pretty ripe by the time we get to the gatehouse."

The guards stopped and searched each traveler. I thought I might scream if they took any longer.

"Come out of your forest for a bit of fun have you?" A guard poked through my bags.

Bix had bundled up fruit on the pretence we were bringing it to Holo to trade. The guard unhooked one of the bags and threw it behind him. I opened my mouth and Rad placed his hand on my arm.

"New fee for entering Holo. This should cover it." The guard smacked my horse's flank. "Be out by nightfall."

And we were through. A sweat broke out over me and I sucked in the hot air.

"Let's check the market and see if we can pick up any word of Caden," Rad said.

The market was still a clamoring, greasy place filled with people trading everything from axes to wooden spoons and noise crashed around us like an orchestra tuning up before a performance.

Rad and I dismounted and guided our horses to a large stable at the far end of the market. Before leading the animals into the dark interior, the stable hand held out his dirty palm and Rad dropped a short length of silver chain into it.

"Need a little extra if you want your bundles to still be here when you come back." The man grinned, showing off an abundance of chipped teeth.

Rad reached into the bag he'd slung over his shoulder and pulled out another length of chain. "You'll bleed me before I even get to market." Rad's voice was light, as if the guy was his dearest friend. "I'd appreciate it if you'd keep the horses ready."

We wandered back into the market. Rad made a point of stopping at all of the carts and tables, gazing over their contents and chatting with the merchants. I knew that he was trying to gather information, but I wanted this over as soon as possible. I was about to pull him away from a particularly in-depth conversation he was having with a woman selling rusty nuts and bolts, when pounding footsteps sounded from one of the narrow passages leading from the market.

Soldiers rushed in, pushing people aside, and Rad grabbed my arm, propelling me into a small, nearby tent. Inside, a scrawny gray-haired woman sat on the bare ground. She turned over a tattered, hand-drawn tarot card and looked up from where she sat with milky-white, unseeing eyes.

"Which of you want a reading?" she asked.

Rad pushed me down. "My sister would like to know what the future holds."

She gathered the cards then looked straight at him. "Why would your sister," she emphasized the word, "be needing a reading? You've got the eye."

"It's one thing for a brother to say, isn't it? She'll believe you before she does me."

She sighed and held out her hand. "Give me your palm." She ran her rough fingers lightly over it, screwing up her face as if listening to some inner voice. "There's something here…no, that can't be!" She dropped my hand. "If this is some kind of trick, you can take it elsewhere."

"There is no trick," Rad said, glancing at the unmarked palm I held up for his inspection.

"I'm seldom mistaken." She picked up her cards and shuffled them with trembling fingers. "We may have better luck with these."

The soldiers passed by the tent, their footsteps scraping across the hard-packed dirt.

"Don't worry, they won't come in here. Scared of me, though I can't imagine why." She dealt out a row of ten ragged cards, and stared down at them as though she could see their faces, before raising her head. "Your future hides behind the tapestry of time. You'll have to give up something because you can't have it all. Nobody can. Can't tell you which to choose either, you'll have to make that decision when it comes." She dealt another row. "There's dark and light, over and over again, this is what I see."

The market noises had returned to their usual clamor.

"We should be going." Rad reached into his bag and brought out a length of silver chain.

The woman shook her head and turned over another row of cards. "When you meet the power, let it drain you. If you fight it, it becomes even more powerful and you become weaker. That's the only way you'll survive and the only way you can get close to the source." She held out her hand to Rad and snatched the chain. "That's it, there isn't any more."

"I don't understand any of it," I said.

"You will," she said. "And if you do survive, which I highly doubt, you can come back and tell me all about it."

The air in the market wasn't much better than the tent. The crowds closed in around us and I wanted to smash my way out.

"What did she mean? Do you think she even knew what she was talking about?" I asked.

"She seemed quite certain."

Rad steered me past a man cooking on an open grill. Behind him, live animals crouched in cramped, wooden cages. I looked away, sickened by the thought of what would happen to them. I stopped.

"I can't let that man cook those animals."

"He's been doing it forever." Rad sighed. "You can't save everything and everyone, Jodi. Leave it."

A voice behind me said, "I'll take this one, yeah, the furry rascal. Cut it up small before you cook it, got a family to feed."

That was too much. I whirled around and stomped toward the cages, my fists clenched. "Excuse me, how much for...my cat!"

Chowder dangled, squirming, by the scruff of her neck. I ripped the customer's fingers away and held her to my chest.

"What is it?" Rad asked.

"That's my cat from outside."

Rad's fingers dug into my arm. "Watch your words."

"It's my meal," the man grasped Chowder's head, "and I'll not go hungry."

"Tell him to take his hands off of her," I cried as Chowder let out a pitiful howl.

"I advise you to let go of the cat." Rad glanced around the market before pulling a knife from the folds of his clothing. He held it to the customer's side. "Now."

The cook stood back, laughing. "I don't care whose cat it is, one of you is going to pay me for it." He slapped a bloody hand on his thigh.

Holding Chowder's small head in his grubby hand, the customer twisted his wrist and I heard a snap. Chowder went limp in my arms.

"You've…you've killed her." I fell to my knees, cradling her body.

"Well, now that I think about it, you know, I don't believe I fancy cat today." The man turned to the cook. "Give me something else."

I had an overwhelming sense of guilt for having allowed Chowder to come to Aten with me. I'd been selfish and stupid and I wanted her back so badly. I looked up as the customer chose another animal for his meal, his murderous act already forgotten. My gut boiled and a fierce rage kicked in. I imagined the guy's face pressed against the steaming grill. His cheeks still glowed with tears of laughter as the cook plucked another poor animal from its cage. The customer nodded and leaned over the hot grill. It would be so easy to simply give him a nudge.

A crowd moved between us, blocking him from view. Then a scream erupted over their heads and the people jumped back, revealing the brute on the ground, moaning and flapping his hands in front of his face. Welts ran across forehead and nose like rivers of red.

"We've got to get out of here." Rad threw a length of silver at the cook.

I stumbled to my feet and pressed my wet face into Chowder's still warm body, her matted fur choking me. Rad led me away from the market and into an alley.

"What's gotten into you? We shouldn't draw attention to ourselves."

"Rad, this is Chowder, my cat from home. And now she's dead." I snorted back the tears and wrapped my fingers around her tiny paw. "She was all I had left."

"All right, all right, we'll take her with us when we leave and give her a nice spot to rest in the forest." He put his arm stiffly around me and patted my back.

Chowder's body lay between us and, when she meowed, Rad's arms tightened and we looked at each other. Drawing apart, I gazed down at Chowder as she crawled up and laid her paws on my shoulder, nuzzling her damp nose against my ear.

"By all that is green, how did that happen?" Rad asked.

My mouth opened and closed and, all the while, my mind raced. The answer was there, but I was almost too frightened to admit knowing it. I took a deep breath.

"When Enrial visited me in my time, she told me I had a special ability, but wouldn't tell me what it was." I thought back to the first time I'd been on Aten. "I know this sounds nuts, it is nuts, but I was able to restore a flower that Neil had mangled and then, when Caden had been injured, no killed, in battle, I was holding his hand when he came back to life. I thought Aladar had used some kind of magic on him, but I think it may have been me."

I also remembered Enrial had told me I had a weakness, but if I could bring people and things back to life, who cared about a weakness?

Rad tapped his finger on his lips. "By the nut, Jodi, the Major may want the key, but if he finds out about this, he would covet your ability above all else."

Chowder's claws dug into my shoulder.

"She went in there," someone shouted.

More yelling, stampeding footsteps and the sense that darkness was coming. Rad pushed me along the alley and around the next bend. A brick wall blocked our path. There was nowhere else to go.

"Get away, Rad, it's me they want."

"Jodi, there are some things we can't change." He pulled out his knife and rushed toward the advancing soldiers.

# Chapter Twelve

The dungeons lay deep under Holo like forgotten rabbit warrens and I was alone, except for a flickering candle and Chowder. She sprawled over my lap, licking and biting the knots tangled in her fur. How she had come to Holo was still a mystery.

The Major's soldiers had far outnumbered Rad and he'd crumpled beneath their clubs and feet. He could have been next door or...no, he wasn't dead. I'd promised him I wouldn't let that happen. The damp underground prison didn't offer much hope of escape—the half-sized door had been bolted after they'd thrown me in and for all I knew, the key may have been tossed away.

I drew my hand along Chowder's fur, marveling that I'd brought her back to life. Me. Was that my ability or merely a coincidence? I hoped I'd never have another opportunity to find out. Chowder wrapped her rough tongue around my fingertips.

"What do we do now?"

Footsteps sounded from the passage. A key scraped in the lock and torchlight penetrated the gloom as the door creaked open. I reached for Chowder then let my hand fall back as she sprang from my lap and shot through the door.

"Out you come," said a tin-pot guard. "Whoa, what was that?"

I pushed up from the ground. Wherever Chowder had taken off to, I hoped she'd find a way out of here and hightail it as far from this place as possible.

"Where are you taking me?" I asked.

"You must be something special, the Major himself is asking to see you."

I staggered against the wall. This was it; the Major had finally caught up to me. I threw back my shoulders. No, I'd caught up with him and I wasn't afraid. Why then did I feel like vomiting? I walked between two guards through the long tunnels. Only weeks before, Nashira had led me through here to an outport we'd used to escape to Nereen. If I could go back to that time, would I change anything?

Everything.

I hung my head as we walked up a steep set of stairs, counting. When I'd reached eighty-nine, we emerged into a wide hall, lit by sunshine streaming through arches running along its length. I peeked over the edge to the courtyard where Neil and I had been auctioned. Caden had saved me that time, but who would save me now? I remembered when Gramps had taught me to swim, he'd said, "When you're out in the middle of the lake, all by your lonesome, you've got to be able to trust in your ability." Thanks, Gramps.

We stopped in front of two large, wooden doors.

"Any last words, Missy?"

I rolled my shoulders, ignoring the tension creeping along my spine, and tried to paste a look of determination on my face.

"You're a brave one." He nodded his head to the other guard. "How long you figure before we have to come back for her body?"

"Enough time for one drink, I'll wager."

The guards swung back the doors and I forced my right foot forward, then my left. Sheer white fabric rippled over the windows and puddled on the floor. Shaggy animal skins were scattered over the red-tiled floor and unlit torches lined the walls. The Major sat behind a marble table, a spoonful of food halfway to his mouth.

"Ah, Jodi, Jodi, Jodi. At last you've arrived."

"Should I feel special because you know my name?"

"I think what you should be feeling is a great deal of fear." He put the spoon down, raised a napkin from the table and patted his thick lips. "Though I shouldn't be surprised by your bravado, you've been enormously lucky so far."

"Luck has nothing to do with it." I clasped my shaking hands behind me.

"On the contrary, luck has everything to do with it. You seem to have the uncanny ability to latch onto the most helpful people."

My heart thumped when he said 'ability'. The skies outside had darkened. Too early for night, was it going to rain?

"What do you want?" I asked.

"You've done something with your hair. Shame." He lumbered around the table. "First, you'll give me the key then you'll accompany me to the archive. Once there, you will open the elevator."

He didn't have the key!

"I can't open the archive," I said.

The Major's face loomed in front of mine. I turned away, but his hand snaked out and he squeezed my chin between his sausage fingers.

"If you don't open the archive, I will find your Dani friends and squash them—for good this time. Not only will I wipe their village off this heap of a planet, I will erase the villagers as well. Do you understand?"

He gave my chin a final squeeze before pushing me away. I stumbled and fell onto the carpet, my eyes stinging with tears. Although I'd always feared the Major, in the back of my mind he'd become an almost comical figure. I touched my chin and realized he wasn't someone to be laughed at.

The Major reached down to the table and lifted something from a silver box. It caught the sunlight and sparkled as he clipped it to his robe. The brooch. My heart was pulled from my chest, dragging me up and forward. I squeezed my eyes shut then remembered the fortune-teller's words: *When you meet the power, let it drain you. If you fight it, it becomes even more powerful.* I floated across the floor toward him, letting the brooch overpower me.

"You know what's good for you, don't you?" His gravelly voice grated in my ears.

I opened my eyes and forced myself to nod.

"Where's the key?" He held out his hand and his palm wavered in and out of focus. "You can give it to me now, I'll take care of it."

I reached down and pulled the necklace from under my clothing—the necklace I'd been given by the woman in Windore. Would he be able to tell it wasn't the real thing? I pulled it over my head and let it sink into his hand.

"That wasn't so hard, was it? You're a good girl, Jodi. I knew you'd see it my way." He held the necklace up, letting the snake charm dangle in front of me. "Seeing how cooperative you've been, I'll let you stay in one of my guestrooms. The cells are far too nasty."

"How do I know you won't hurt the Dani even if I do open the archive?"

"You don't. Get plenty of rest tonight because we'll be taking a journey tomorrow and my soldiers will accompany us, so don't even think about planning an escape enroute."

He picked up something from the table, shook it and the gentle tinkle of a bell sounded. The guards sped into the room, their eyes wide. Amazed to find me alive, I supposed.

"Take her to a guestroom," the Major said.

I stood, not wanting to leave and the Major smiled.

"Don't be discouraged, dear girl, it's the brooch that captivates you. I'd like to think it was me, but, alas, I know where the attraction lies." He angled his head, a questioning look in his eyes. "You truly don't know, do you? It's a tool, created by the same being who created you. She really should've taken better care of it."

He unclipped the brooch and laid it in the box once again. I fell back as though gravity had released me and turning, ran to the guards.

* * * *

I felt like Rapunzel, locked up in her tower, lacking only the long hair and prince to save me. I pulled a bench close to the open window and stared over the dusty town. Peeking out from behind the clouds, the sun set on the wagons and carts traveling up the long road and the Awes forest shone far in the distance—the only spot of life near this dismal place. I closed my eyes and hugged my knees against my chest.

What would happen when we reached the archive? Would the Major kill me when he discovered the key was a fake? I wandered over to the table and nibbled on the food the guards had brought, avoiding the meat and eating only the rice and vegetables.

The single bed, opposite the window, was layered with scratchy blankets and a feather mattress that cushioned me when I slipped between the covers. My eyelids felt as though someone had sewn them shut, but my mind was playing leapfrog as it bounced from one thought to the next—Rad, Caden, Stala, Chowder, the key, the archive, everything except the Major's revelation that I was created.

In the darkness, something brushed over the floor. I gripped the blankets tightly in my fingers and leaned forward, trying to pinpoint where the sound came from. Then a shadow pounced on my bed.

"Chowder!" I reached out my hand and felt her warmth. "How did you find me? Come here."

I dragged her to my chest and rubbed my cheek against her long fur.

"You need a bath." I was in the midst of petting her when I felt something on her tail. "What've you got tangled in this time?"

I picked her up, took her to the bench by the window and, in the light of the moon, worked at the vine circling her tail. A small square of paper fell and, after unfolding an old, hand-made tarot card, I read the words scratched across the worn surface.

*Archive love r*

Archive lover? No, there was a space between the word love and the letter r. It must've been from Rad, for he was the only one who could read. I smiled and pressed the old card against my chest. He was free. I couldn't imagine the fortune-teller had been willing to give up her card, so why had she done it?

I went to the table and pushed my finger into a beet. Back at the window, I wrote the word Yes underneath Rad's note before twisting the card back into the vine and attaching it to Chowder's neck.

"Take this to Rad," I said. Was it possible she understood? It didn't matter, as long as she left. "And get away from Holo, okay?"

I held her soft head in my hands, scratching behind her ears. I might never see her again.

"Go!"

She leapt onto the wide brick of the opening and looked back once before springing out. I heard a scrape, then nothing. Cats always landed on their feet; she'd be all right. I had to believe it.

I didn't bother getting back into bed; I wasn't sure I'd ever sleep again. Sitting on the hard bench and gazing into the cold night, I thought about how the fortuneteller had talked about light and dark and how I'd have to choose.

# Chapter Thirteen

A guard leered down at me, his fingers hovering over my hair. I sat up and slapped his hand. I must've crawled into bed at some point during the night.

"No need for that." He shoved his hands into his pockets. "Rise and smile, Missy, the Major wants you to join him for morning meal."

I slipped on the soft form-fitting boots the Awes had given me, and preceded the guard down the hallway to the double doors. He eased one of them open and I crept through. The Major stood by an arched window, a pair of what looked like binoculars held to his eyes. He lowered them and turned to me.

"It's a good day to travel," he said.

"Are you using the brooch to take us there?" I'd seen the Major disappear once after touching the brooch on his chest and figured it had the same power as my charm.

"I prefer to have my soldiers with us in case there's a surprise waiting at the archive. Obviously the brooch can't take everyone there." He waved his weighty arm over one of the chairs by the marble table. "Come, eat."

"I'm not hungry."

"You prove nothing by your stubbornness. Eat and we'll have a chat."

My stomach rumbled and I sat, pulling a chair closer to a plate filled with steaming biscuits and red berries. I couldn't resist the homey smell of the biscuits and dipped one into the fruit before raising it to my mouth.

"I've waited for this moment a long time." The Major settled across from me with an almost fatherly smile plastered on his face. "Do you know, many of your generations ago, my assistant and I arrived on Aten with big dreams, determined to do everything we could to help your world? Are you shocked to learn I'm not a native of this planet?"

My gaze worked its way from his bulbous face to his door-sized chest then back again. I shook my head, but didn't let on that the revelation of his age astounded me.

"I came here with the Nera."

I swallowed then coughed, trying to dislodge a berry that was caught halfway down my throat.

"You'd better get used to my little surprises," he passed me a cup of water, "because you're in for many more. I was a supply officer in the first wave sent here. It didn't take me long to realize there was power to be had for those willing to take it. I was willing."

My stomach churned. I slapped my hand over my mouth as a ferocious burp escaped, then wiped my forehead and took another drink of water.

"Why are you telling me this?" I whispered.

He leaned forward and tapped a pudgy finger on the table.

"I want you to know that the Nera are not what they appear."

His face blurred and I didn't have the energy to bring it back into focus.

"I feel sick." I laid my head on the table. The marble surface was like an ice pack, soothing and cool. If I didn't move, there was a good chance my breakfast would stay put. A bell tinkled in the distance.

"Yes, Sir?" said a voice behind me.

"Remove her to the guestroom and summon the healer, the one who was here earlier. Quickly, she can't have gone far."

I tried to smile. The Major sounded repelled, and for some reason, that made me happy. Rough hands gripped my arms and pulled me from the chair. If I was going to heave, I really ought to do it here because I would've liked to leave the Major a little gift, but all that came up was another burp. My feet mopped the floor as I was dragged back to my room then thrown onto the bed. I curled up, trying to find a position that would make my stomach feel better. I knew if I opened my eyes, the room would be spinning.

"Leave us." A kind voice. A woman's voice.

A cool hand touched my forehead. Heavenly.

"You'll feel better as soon as you drink this." She raised my head. "I'm sorry you had to go through that, but it was all I could think of to get you alone."

A cup forced my lips open. I gagged, but the woman continued to pour thick, minty stuff down my throat. She eased my head back onto the bed then wiped my face with a damp cloth. The gurgles in my stomach quieted and I risked opening my eyes.

"Juna?"

"The one and only. How are you feeling?"

"Did you poison me?"

The Nera's healer smiled at me. "I bribed the guard who serves the morning meal. The Major should be feeling the effects of my ingredients soon and, hopefully, it'll slow him down for a while."

"What are you doing here?" I'd last seen her after the battle in Nereen where Neil and I had helped stitch up the wounded.

"I was..." Juna hesitated, "I came to trade, but when I heard you'd been taken in, I thought you might need some help."

I swung my feet over the side of the bed. Whatever medicine Juna had given me, it made me feel better than I had when I'd first awakened. "How will we get out of Holo?"

"You are now my apprentice." She poked through a bag on the floor and whipped out a long, gray cape. "Put this on and pull up the hood."

"We'll have to get past the guards first," I said.

"Don't worry about them, they're as good as gone." Juna threw her own cape over her shoulders. Attached to her belt was a silver canister.

"Is that your man-eating dust?"

She laughed and pulled on a pair of tight, black gloves. "You could call it that."

During the battle, the Nera had sprinkled the stuff over the dead and dying enemy. It was an efficient method of disposal because it devoured anything organic, leaving only a black patch.

"I don't want to watch."

"You may not have any choice. Let's go." She took a scoopful of the fine, glittery dust and opened the door.

A guard, leaning against the wall, bounded up.

"How is she?" His last words—he simply disappeared before my eyes.

"Isn't there something else you could've done, something to put him to sleep?" I asked.

"Leave no witnesses," Juna said.

We sped down the hall to the stairs. The Major must have felt very secure in his fortress, for we met no other guards until we reached a small door, several levels down.

"Whoa, seems there was only one of you when you came in. What's going on?" The guard scratched under his tin-pot hat as though he might find the answer there.

Juna doused him in the dust. The guard's hat clanked to the ground, rolling a few meters before it stopped. She reached over the spot where he'd been to open the door and we rushed outside.

"We go slow from here on in. Act as though you belong and never mention the Nera—these people believe me to be a healer and nothing else." Juna gingerly peeled off the gloves and tucked them into a pocket in her cape. "We'll make our way to the gatehouse and wait until a crowd is leaving."

I pulled the hood down over my face, keeping my gaze on the hem of Juna's cape. The noise of the market thundered, insulating us from prying eyes as we stopped at a stall and fingered the rotting vegetables on display before moving on. It was an agonizing trip and each second I expected to hear the harsh yells of the guards or soldiers. How long would it take before my absence was noticed?

We waited at the end of the market until a group of people passed by on their way out of Holo, and Juna and I fell in behind them. The guards seemed less concerned with those leaving than those heading into town and we were waved through. We didn't speak until we were halfway up the dusty road.

"We can't leave. Not until we find Caden," I said.

"Caden isn't here."

"Do you know that for sure?" I glanced back at the town. "He could be in the dungeons."

"The dungeons would never hold him."

"I got a note from Rad." Rad would help me find Caden, I was sure of it. "Have you seen him?"

"The seer, Lurren, saw him leave last night."

"If Caden isn't here, then I've got to go to the archive; that's where Rad will be," I said.

"No, we've got to take you out of the equation. Without you, the archive can't be opened. Where's the key?"

Juna's gaze bored into me, almost as though she could probe my mind. The Major had said *'I want you to know that the Nera are not what they appear'*. What were they then?

"I lost it."

"You lost it? It was your responsibility to keep it safe." Juna massaged her forehead. "It's unfortunate we weren't aware of the key before, we would have secured the archive and kept it safe from the Major."

"How did you find out I had it?"

"When we realized who and what the Major was looking for. Up until then, we thought you a simple outsider." She frowned. "The Mother could've let us in on the secret."

The road was steep and we stopped talking, saving our breath for the exhausting trip. Too much information was rattling around in my head, all of it conflicting. I couldn't trust the Major, but could I trust the Nera? The Major didn't have the key, so what had happened to Catta? And Caden wasn't in Holo. Juna's lips pressed tightly together, looking determined to take me out of the equation. Rad had suggested I must decide what was most important to me. I closed my eyes and cleared my mind, focusing on the sun beating down upon my head. So what was my priority?

Rad. He'd seen only darkness after Holo. His darkness. I had to get to the archive, but that meant escaping from the woman who'd saved me.

"Where are we going?" I asked.

"We've a camp set up outside the forest. We'll stay there tonight and then you'll be taken to Nereen and kept there."

Had the Major been telling the truth? The Nera had always been kind to me, so why was I filled with doubt? Was there anyone I could trust? In my heart, I knew the answer—three brothers, Caden, Rad and Aladar—and it was to them I owed my allegiance. I smiled at Juna.

"I can't wait to see everyone in Nereen."

# Chapter Fourteen

By the time we reached the edge of the Awes forest, the sun dazzled high in the sky and despite the enforced illness I'd been through, my stomach was begging to be fed. Juna led me along the cliffs of Deakin Canyon until we came to a secluded spot, surrounded by the overhanging branches of the forest and the gray boulders atop the canyon. She waved her hand and an opening appeared, revealing the Nera's camp. Like Nereen, an invisible barrier protected it. Erected in the middle of the space was a small, circus-type tent.

"We've set up a barrier on the this side only, so be careful near the canyon. The others must still be in town." She looked around, then sat down, stretching her arms over her head. "I'm certainly not up for that kind of excitement anymore."

The Major had implied that he and the Nera had arrived here hundreds of years ago. Juna had a few lines around her eyes, but, surely, she couldn't be that old—aliens were supposed to look like the Major, but all the Nera were beautiful.

"Is Nashira here with you?" I asked.

"No, she's in Nereen."

Escape would be easier without Nashira's sharp eyes over-seeing everything, and those here wouldn't expect me to try and make a getaway. But with the barrier in place between Holo and the camp, I could only go through the canyon.

"Are you hungry?" Juna disappeared into the tent and returned carrying a cloth sack. She drew out a handful of dried fruits then passed the sack to me.

"Thanks." I nibbled at the wrinkled fruit, occasionally flicking my gaze over the camp. Going to the archive through the canyon wouldn't be an easy thing to attempt alone during the day and almost impossible at night.

"Have you seen Aladar?" I asked.

She shook her head.

The lonely clip-clop of a horse's hooves echoed up from below. There must have been a nearby path leading from the canyon. I jumped up, looking for a place to hide and Juna laughed.

"Don't worry," she said. "It's an old friend."

As the steps neared, a pleasant whistling sailed from the canyon. A few minutes later, with a line of fish in one hand and leading his horse with another, Neil popped into view. I held my hands over my mouth.

Dressed in a woven jacket and dusty, black pants, he was no longer a naïve sixteen-year-old; Neil had shot up in height. On his chin, a blond beard grew thick and wild, and his hair reached his broad shoulders. In the short time I'd been away from Aten, Neil had become a man.

He gave the fish to Juna before spotting me. Stopping, one foot poised above the ground, his mouth gaped. Then he was beside me, looking down at me with the same blue eyes I remembered.

"You're back." His deep voice was almost unrecognizable.

"You've changed." I held him at arm's length. "You've grown up without me."

"Never stopped thinking about you, though." He held my hands, his own were rough and calloused. "Except for the hair color, you haven't changed at all."

"That's because, as far as my time is concerned, I saw you about a week ago. I'm still sixteen and you, you're eighteen." I laughed. "An old man."

We continued staring at one another until Neil looked away, his cheeks pink.

I nodded my head away from the camp. "Let's talk over there." We settled, cross-legged on the moss beside the forest. Behind him, Juna puttered in front of her tent.

"Neil, we don't have time to waste. We've got to get out of here, but," I looked over his shoulder, "we can't let Juna know we're going."

"Why not?" Would I ever get used to that deep voice?

"She wants to hide me away in Nereen, but I've got to meet Rad at the archive."

"Rad now, is it?" He looked at my neck. "Where's the necklace?" I explained the situation to him. "I didn't tell Juna about Catta."

"You don't trust her?"

"Other than Aladar and Rad, I don't know who I can trust anymore."

A flash of anger lit his eyes. "You can trust me."

"I didn't mean you. Oh, I'm so sick of it. All I seem to do is run around, trying to find answers and only getting into more trouble." I gazed into my lap. "And I'm tired of pretending to be brave."

"We'll leave tonight, but you're going to have to be brave some more," he whispered. "The way to the archive can be dangerous."

Before going to bed, Neil tethered his horse close to the canyon path. We huddled under our covers in the darkness and waited until we heard mellow snores coming from the tent. My nerves were stretched to the breaking point, so I was happy when Neil gave the sign it was time to pack up.

The moss near the forest muffled our footsteps as we tiptoed to the canyon. As Neil led the horse down the path, he stroked its neck and whispered comforting though incoherent words. When we reached the canyon floor, we climbed onto the horse and I wedged my legs through the bulky bags and coiled rope that cluttered its sides.

"You're a bit paranoid if you think the Nera mean you any harm," Neil said.

"It's not that they want to hurt me, they want to keep me safe. At least, their idea of safe." I laid my cheek against his back. "I have too many things to do."

"You just don't want to miss out on any of the fun."

"I wouldn't exactly call my adventures here a party."

The river rolled alongside of us and the moon peeked overhead, shedding a dim light on our path.

"Tell me about the last couple of years," I said.

Neil described traveling with his dad and going farther and farther each time they ventured out. They never got into the archive, though they did try. Lately, he'd been going out on his own.

"We made Kopi our home base because of all the tools and stuff Dad can use."

"Where is he?"

"Last I heard, he was headed to Nereen to get the outports working again, but I think it's beyond even his ability."

I slid forward as we rode down a steep hill. The river rumbled over the height and sprayed us with a frosty mist.

"Are you happy here?"

"Things have changed, I've changed, but I made the right decision." He paused. "How's my mom?"

"I told her you wouldn't be coming back and that you were with your dad. You've got to remember, I left the same night I told her, so I don't know how she's doing now. Sorry."

"She'll understand. She knew why my dad decided to stay here, so she'll figure out why I did, too." Neil sighed, then in a stronger voice he said, "We'll put as much distance as we can between the Nera and us, then grab a few hours of sleep."

I don't know how long we rode before Neil decided to call it a night, but I did discover it's an easy thing falling asleep on a horse.

"Must've been tired." I wiped the sleep from my eyes then watched as Neil laid out the bedding. Once the sun set, Deakin Canyon became refrigerator cold, so it would be nice to get under the warmth of the blankets. "How long till morning?"

"Two hours or so, then we'll have to get moving."

"You seem so much a part of Aten now," I said. "Do you even remember what it was like back home?"

"I can only remember the last couple of years there and how unhappy I was with my dreams and Dad gone. Do I miss stuff like T.V., fast food or good music? Yeah, lots."

"I brought my knapsack and some tunes, but I lost them in the Kurage's underground caves." Bit by bit I was losing what remained of my world.

"Met up with those bowls of jelly, did you? Maybe one day we'll rescue it 'cause I'd sure like to hear some real music."

Somewhere along the canyon's cliffs, there was an arch, and through the arch there was a pool, and through the pool there was a cave, and through the cave there was Stala. If she'd escaped the glowing, green darkness of the Phosphor Caves once, couldn't she do it again? When I retrieved my knapsack, I'd save Stala, too. I frowned. I'd better make a list of all the things I hoped to achieve—they were starting to add up.

Neil slept, his breath even and shallow. I hooked my arms behind my head and stared at the sky. Hidden under the same stars, were all the answers as well as all the problems. A wave of giddiness hit me and I clamped my hand over my mouth to smother the giggles. And there I was, Jodi Greer, thinking I could solve everything.

Neil shook me. "We've got to get going."

"Okay, okay. What time is it?" I squinted against a dawn sky that was just beginning to brighten.

"Time, Jodi? We don't have time on Aten. There's morning, noon and night. Here, catch." He tossed an apple to me. "Once we're out of the canyon, we'll go through a pass I discovered."

"Not the Chuma Pass." I pressed my palm against my chest. "We'd never get through alive."

"There's another pass through the Jagger Hills that'll take us closer to the archive." Neil helped me onto the horse then climbed up in front. "I've discovered a lot about this place while you've been gone."

When we'd first come to Aten, Neil had needed me. Things had turned around and I wasn't sure how I felt about it. Everyone here thought they knew what was best for me and, as clueless as I might've been, I didn't like giving up control. I shivered. Even the colorful walls of the canyon couldn't brighten the day. Clouds scudded overhead and I wrapped the blanket around my shoulders, keeping it there as we rode.

"So what else did this Enrial woman tell you?"

"That I was able to travel here alone and I was supposed to turn this world around. Made sense at the time, now it just sounds nuts."

"She didn't say anything else?" he asked.

I stared at Neil's back. His shoulders and neck looked tense as though he were holding his breath.

"Nothing else."

Neil was my oldest friend; I'd shared everything with him since we were kids. Why wasn't I sharing the news of my so-called ability? Was I afraid he'd laugh? Neil was right—I was paranoid—my paranoia meter was off the scale. A cold wind snaked through the canyon and I let go of his waist, grasping the blanket tightly with my icy fingers.

If the Nera tried to follow us, they hadn't yet succeeded in catching up. What had they thought when they'd found us gone? Somehow I imagined Juna wouldn't easily give up on me. I tried sorting out all the secrets I'd withheld over the past week and realized I was as bad as Rad, making everything a mystery. Maybe being on Aten kicked in some self-preservation strategy for me, making it impossible to tell the whole truth and nothing but the truth.

"What's going to happen when we get to the archive?" Neil steered the horse along the narrow path. "We can't get in without the charm."

"I promised Rad I'd meet him there." Without revealing Rad's vision of what he believed to be his own death, it was impossible to explain.

"You got something going with Rad? What happened to Caden?"

"I've got to find Caden, too."

The horse jerked to a stop and whinnied. Despite digging his heels into its belly, Neil couldn't make the animal go around the next bend. We slid quietly down.

"Wait here."

Neil crouched down and pressed against the rock before disappearing from sight. I hesitated for a moment then crept along the canyon wall and taking a deep breath, poked my head around the bend.

# Chapter Fifteen

Neil knelt by the remains of a fire, picking through the debris. He stuffed something into his pocket and whipped around when my boots grated over the loose stones.

"Don't come any closer."

"What is it?" I took another step into the small clearing and gasped at the sight that had, seconds before, been hidden from view.

A man's body sagged, tied by his wrists between two scrawny pine trees. His chin pressed into his chest and slashes of blood snaked across his pale arms. I turned my face away, waiting for the wave of nausea to pass. Neil's footsteps scraped across the clearing.

"Do you know who it is?" I asked.

"Yes." Neil's hand caressed my back. "And so do you."

I squeezed my eyes shut. "Who?"

"It's Paul."

"Is he dead?" Of course he was dead, no one could look more dead than he did. Pushing past Neil, I ran to Paul and touched his hand. So cold. I curled my fingers around his and tried to summon whatever part of me could bring people back to life. There were no sounds in the deep canyon—no birds, no rumbling river nearby. I waited for his breath, but only a steady silence filled the air. Releasing Paul's stiff fingers, I pounded on his chest and his head swung around, lifeless still.

"What are you doing?" Neil yanked me away. "Have you completely lost it, Jodi?"

"He should be alive!"

"Of course he should be alive," Neil said. "But he's dead and there isn't anything we can do about it."

I rubbed my eyes. What had gone wrong? Did my ability only work with certain people or things?

"How long has he been dead?" I asked.

Neil's index finger disappeared into his beard as he scratched his chin. "I don't know, no more than a day or else the wolves and crows would've..."

"Okay, you don't have to give me the details, I get the idea."

Maybe there was a time frame I had to work within, an hour, maybe even twenty-four, but no more. How many hours had Rad been away from Holo? I tried to concentrate. I'd received the note from him two nights ago.

"We've got to get to the archive." I grabbed Neil's arm. "How long till we get there?"

"Unless we run into trouble, about two days."

Two days. Would I be too late? I wiped my hands on my pants and bit my lip. There was nothing I could do to slow down time.

"I guess we should take care of Paul before we go." I swallowed, wondering if I'd ever erase the image of his lifeless body from my mind. The first morning in Kopi, Paul had been kind to me. I grasped that memory and held it.

We piled rocks and stones over Paul and said a few words before turning away. Neil had finally convinced his horse to come into the clearing and now slipped his jacket under one of the bundles.

"You think Arax killed him?" he asked.

"Once Paul helped him escape from Kopi, Arax probably tortured him until he found out where the archive was."

As Neil led the horse away, I glanced back at the pile of gray rocks that already looked as though they'd been there a lifetime. Paul really should have been happy with simply teaching Rad to read.

Along the pebbly path, the sun made an appearance, though by that time I'd already worked up a good sweat by heaping rocks over Paul. I moved to the other side of the horse, into the shade, and my foot slipped.

"Neil, look at this." I bent and held up a beaded leather pouch. "Do you know who this belongs to?"

He shook his head.

"Catta! I saw her wearing it when I first got back to Aten and she put my necklace inside." I ripped the pouch open. Empty. "This might mean Arax has Catta."

"And the key. I can't let Arax get in there! What he doesn't understand, he destroys and that would be everything inside the archive." Neil slammed his fist into his hand.

"It doesn't matter, he can't get in. I'm the only one who can open it."

"Then the archive is still safe." Neil paced up and down the narrow path. "When we get there, you're going to have to hide while I get the key from him."

"What about Rad?" I threw the useless pouch on the ground.

"Why are you so worried about him? Rad is more than capable of taking care of himself." Neil mounted the horse, then pulled me up.

A few hours later, we trudged out of Deakin Canyon, leading the horse behind us. I tried to shake off the dust and weariness, knowing I'd need every bit of energy and bravery to confront whoever waited at the archive. It bothered me that Neil and I hadn't spoken much all day. How could I not have a million things to say to my oldest friend?

We reached the plateau we'd camped on the first time we'd been on Aten. A narrow tract of land, trapped between the canyon and the Jagger Hills, the dry, cracked earth seemed to have been alternatively squeezed then torn apart.

"I won't be able to find the pass at night," Neil said. "I've only used it once before."

"Do you remember the last time we were here?" I pointed at a stand of scraggly pines poking up in the distance. "You'd been stung by the Hachi and I wasn't sure if you'd ever wake up. When you did, we were Arax's prisoners."

"That was a long time ago." Neil shook his head. "The Hachi wouldn't catch me off guard this time and neither would Arax."

We set up camp by the trees as they offered some protection from the autumn winds blowing across the plateau. After eating nuts mixed in a watery porridge, we settled down for the night. Even though the Awes' clothing protected me from the elements, the cold air was insistent, and I lay back, tugging the blankets over me. The night sky blossomed above us, flashing streaks of purples and pinks.

"Hey, Neil, the Northern Lights."

"That's been happening a lot lately. Dad says it's because Earth's magnetic fields have flipped."

"Wow, it's spectacular. It's amazing how much has changed." I shifted in the blankets, trying to find a more comfortable spot. There wasn't one. "Like you."

Neil grunted. "Everything changes. You should get some rest."

The lights shimmered and slid over the sky like beautiful dancers in an otherwise dingy theatre. A lump settled in my throat and I felt tears seeping from the corners of my eyes. Other than the colorful skies, there was no beauty here, only greed and savagery. How could Enrial believe I was capable of bringing this world back on track when I couldn't even get a handle on my own feelings of hopelessness? Everyone on Aten was simply struggling to survive. I looked up at the sky.

"Somebody," I whispered, "please help me make the right decisions."

"You were sure tossing and turning last night," I said.

"Me?" Neil stroked his beard. "Guess I've got lots on my mind."

"Like what?"

"Like what I'm going to do when I catch up with Arax. Here, help me get this stuff folded."

It was still so early, the sun had barely put in an appearance, yet I felt more alert than I'd been for the past week. I put my hands on my hips.

"Neil, what's wrong? You've changed so much."

"You've been gone for over two years, what did you expect?"

"I expected to find my old friend. Remember him? He's the guy who used to stand by my side when all the other little kids made fun of my red hair. The one I built a tree fort with and shared my poems with. Where is he?"

Neil's back was to me, but it didn't hide the fact that my words had knocked the wind out of him. His shoulders slumped.

"I wish he were here, Jodi, but he's not." Neil turned around, his face pale. "When you get the necklace back, open the archive and then go home. I don't want you to end up like me. Okay?"

"No, it's not okay because I don't understand." I rushed to him and gripped his arms.

He peeled my hands away and placed them at my sides. His face was so incredibly sad, if I'd had the necklace right then, I would've found a way to take us both home.

"This is who I am now. I'm not the skinny kid who lives down the street from you anymore. I am what Aten made me."

"What happened while I was gone?" I rubbed the spots on my arms where Neil had held them.

"Jodi, stop. Let's just get through this and, I promise I'll make sure nothing happens to you."

We climbed onto the horse and rode beside the Jagger Hills, veering around the entrance to the Chuma Pass where the wind whistled from the opening. Was it the sound of all the voices that had been silenced there over the years? I leaned against Neil, glad he knew of another path through the Hills—not only would we avoid the Chuma, we'd stay clear of the Hachi lurking on the other side.

The basketball-sized spiders the people here called the Hachi terrorized a small section of forest. Their sticky webs had dropped down on Neil and me within minutes of our arrival the first time we'd visited Aten and even though I knew I'd never have to tackle them again, a shiver ran up my back and continued along my arms—nothing could persuade me to go back in there.

The sun crept up our backs as we followed the hills. When it threatened to shine in our eyes, Neil pulled on the reins and brought our horse to a stop.

"I think the path is just ahead. Let's eat before we go in."

While Neil dug through one of his bags, I kicked at tufts of shriveled grass and wondered how long it would be before winter set in. We leaned our backs against the cold rocks as we ate, but after a few moments silence, I coughed. Neil looked up at me.

"Have you ever figured out where the magic comes from?" I asked.

"I guess that woman, Enrial, had something to do with it. Or maybe the Nera."

"But why? Why didn't they just leave Earth as it was?" I wiped the crumbs from my palms. "If Enrial has such great powers, what does she expect me to do? Why doesn't she just help Aten herself?"

"Maybe she just wanted to give the people here something to work with. Maybe she picked your name out of a hat. There could be hundreds of people like you here, all trying to make Aten a better place. They could all have a key to the archive." He shrugged. "Hell, maybe this isn't the only archive on Aten."

There were probably more dream travelers like Neil, his dad and Paul, so there might be more people like me. But Enrial had said I was the only one. Had she been telling the truth?

As the sun beat a hasty retreat, I tried not to show my impatience as Neil searched for his pass through the hills. When I was about to suggest we should go another way, he let out a triumphant yell and signaled me over to a meter-wide fissure in the rock that was well hidden by brush and scrub.

The path inside was narrow and winding—too narrow for us to ride the horse. We walked slowly around darkening bends and under rocky arches while talking about old times—teachers we'd liked, our favorite hangouts around town and friends we'd partied with. I was thankful to catch a glimpse of the old Neil as well as take my mind off Rad.

"Hey, what was the date when you left?" Neil asked.

I tried to remember the date I'd put on my letter to Gramps. It seemed so long ago. "July twenty-third."

"So it might be August ninth right about now. Happy birthday."

My seventeenth birthday. Back home, I'd have been calling friends and arranging a party. On Aten, I was simply hoping to survive one more day.

Farther along, the path widened into a small oasis. Visible through the approaching dusk, water bubbled over a cliff and fell into a small, dark pond. Trees and ferns gathered tightly around the far edge as though jostling for position at a parade, while butterflies floated over the spray of water like tiny, wayward balloons. I felt cushioned and safe for the first time in days.

"Funny," he said, "I thought there were more trees."

"Are you feeling okay?" I frowned. "It's beautiful in here."

"Yeah, if you like rocks. I figured there had to be another pass through the hills." Neil nodded his head, wearing the first real smile I'd seen on him since we'd left the Nera's camp. "It might be a bit uncomfortable but I think it's safe. We'll stay here tonight."

"I've got to get to the archive."

"It'll be dark soon." He pulled one of the sacks off the horse. "I don't want to go near the archive at night."

"Rad might be in trouble."

"Would you stop with Rad already? I'll go up the path a bit and gather some dry wood if I can find any." Neil lit a long torch and stuck the base between two rocks before taking his lamp and wandering farther down the path.

Why couldn't Neil appreciate the beauty of this place? I gazed at the pond, suddenly aware of my dirty hair and hands. After glancing over my shoulder, I slipped out of my clothes and dipped my toe into the pool. Cold, but the promise of feeling clean was too tempting. I waded in until I was half submerged, then scrubbed my face and neck. I heard Neil dump the wood but I ignored him and leaned back, waving my hair in the water until my head became numb from the cold. It felt great.

"Can you throw me a blanket?" I called. "Neil?"

I turned toward the campsite, but darkness had descended, making it impossible to see anything. I peered into the gloom, looking for the slightest flash of the torch or Neil's lamp. Nothing.

"Neil?" I whispered.

I crossed my arms over my chest and twirled around in the water. The tip of a fern touched my shoulder and I reeled toward the shore, a cowardly scream hiding in my throat. My clothes stuck to my wet arms and legs as I stumbled into them. I was afraid to call his name again, afraid to call attention to myself.

I couldn't see my fingers in front of me as I padded the air with my hands, hoping to feel the softness of our horse. I touched the cold, rocky wall and turned, determined to find something familiar. It was at that moment I saw lights deep within the trees on the other side of the pond. I watched them for a few moments before deciding it couldn't be Neil's lamp because it didn't flicker or move.

I don't know how long I stood there waiting for Neil to come back, but finally my wet clothes and the cold air prompted me to take a step toward the lights. Then another. I plowed through the ferns, stopping every once in awhile by a tree to find the courage to get closer. I'd probably gone less than fifty meters when I came to the light's source and the sight astounded me.

A cottage that could've come straight out of an English countryside was ablaze with a warm glow pouring from both its frosted windows. A cheery brick walk meandered through a garden to a door standing slightly ajar, inviting me to come in.

Why hadn't Neil told me about this place? I tiptoed to one of the windows but was unable to see past the intricate frosted design. Was he inside? As much as I wanted to find out, I couldn't move from the front step. Nothing I'd seen on Aten had prepared me for something as normal as this cottage.

"You'd better come in and dry off," said a familiar voice.

# Chapter Sixteen

I stepped through the door and into a sitting room where Enrial sat in an overstuffed chair. A delicate floral teapot and two cups were placed on a small table in front of her and leaning forward, she filled the cups with steaming brown liquid. She glanced at me, and I was again struck by her ageless beauty.

"Tea?" she asked.

"What are you doing here?" I threw my hands wide. "What is this cottage doing here?"

"Quaint, isn't it?" Enrial pointed to a chair opposite her. "Please, sit down and let the fire warm you."

I glanced at the fireplace as I slid into the chair then continued looking around the cottage.

"Those lights are electric," I said.

"For your benefit. I thought you might enjoy a touch from home." She sat back, holding the saucer and cup in her hand. "Now, tell me what you've been up to."

"I have a feeling you already know."

"Not true—I can't keep an eye on what's happening all the time. That's what you're here for."

"Where's Neil?"

"Outside, gathering wood."

I leaned back in the chair, the thick cushion swallowing me, and a wave of exhaustion caught me. I let my eyes close, knowing that with Enrial nearby, both Neil and I were safe.

"Jodi," she said, "I'm afraid I can't stay long."

"I'm so tired."

She nodded. "Drink up, it'll make you feel better."

"What am I supposed to do here?" I took the handle of the dainty cup between my thumb and index finger and drank the contents in a few gulps. "I'm just one person. And what's with the Major? Why don't you do something about him?"

"I can't."

"But you said you could control everything but me. You said—."

She raised her palm to stop me.

"Our plans were put into place long ago—the archive, you and the necklace, the dream travelers, the Nera—everything we could think of to help. Tuldume, or the Major as you call him, was not part of our plans and there's nothing I can do about him now."

"Then you lied."

She shrugged. "Call it what you will, I needed to say something to give you a bit of encouragement to return to Aten."

"If you can make this," I waved my arm, "then you can give the people here everything they need."

She sighed. "All an illusion, I'm afraid. Our job is done."

"And what do you expect me to do?"

"You must take control of the archive. Afterward, should the need arise, gather together the children of the Nera because with them, you'll have the power to overcome any enemy and move this world forward." She set down her cup. "You've been spending far too much time trying to recover what you've lost."

I turned away. "You know about the necklace."

"And your cat, and your friends and everything else you've mislaid." She sounded exasperated. "We gave you the tools to succeed, but perhaps you still need time to fully appreciate them. As much as I know your heart will tell you the right thing to do, I'm afraid you're not doing it quite as quickly as we'd like."

"The Major thinks I have an uncanny ability to latch onto helpful people. Is that just a coincidence or do you have something to do with it?"

"I can only point you in the right direction, it's up to you to go forward."

"You also gave me the ability to bring people back to life." Remembering Rad, I rose from the chair and paced in front of the fire. "I need to find Rad."

"I need you to do the job you were sent here to do. Each season, this world strays further from salvation."

"I can't do what you ask."

"Can't or won't?" Enrial frowned. "I'd hoped you would at least try, but if you're not willing, we'll have to rely on our other options."

"You said there weren't any more like me."

Enrial took my hand then steered me toward the door.

"Not exactly like you, no, but we couldn't depend only on your success." She stepped back and pushed me into the doorway. "Against the objections of the others, I insisted on adding you to the mix. I'm sorry, Jodi, but I can no longer continue to defend your lack of action."

I shoved the books into my locker, closing the door quickly before they tumbled out. Beside me, Lisa Gantry balanced her own books on her hip as she flipped her lock open, but there were too many and the books tumbled to the ground. I bent and helped her pick them up.

"Thanks, Jodi. Hey, how was your summer?"

"Boring." I stared at the book clutched in my hand—*Brave New World*.

"Are you reading that one too?" Lisa asked.

I shook my head and handed the book to her. "For a minute there, I just thought...it doesn't matter."

"Want to come to the coffee shop after school? There's a bunch of us going."

"I have to go home."

"Your mom?" I hated the look of pity on her face.

"Got some stuff to do." I started to turn away.

"Where's Neil? I haven't seen him since we got back."

I stared at her, my mind blank.

"You okay?" she asked.

"Yeah, I guess I'm tired—not used to getting up early." I smiled, trying to cover up the empty feeling inside before walking toward my next class. Neil. Where was he? We'd hardly spoken for the last few years, yet I missed him terribly. Maybe I'd drop by his house on the way home.

Mrs. Moran stood on the porch as a man hammered a *For Sale* sign in her lawn. I watched for a moment then walked slowly up the path.

"Are you moving?"

"Of course," she said.

"Is that why Neil isn't at school?"

A motorcycle raced down the street, its engines filling the void of silence. Mrs. Moran's eyebrows bunched together and she angled her head.

"You told me a few weeks ago that he wouldn't be coming back," she said.

For the past week it had been like that—fuzzy and disconnected, people saying things that either didn't make sense or that my mind would shut out.

"I don't know what you mean. How could I know he's not coming back if I don't even know where he is?"

Like Lisa, Mrs. Moran shot me a look of pity.

"You should go home, Jodi." She dug her hands into her apron pockets. "Everybody should go home."

I backed away from her, glancing only once at the sign on her lawn. Even if we hadn't hung out for a long time, the least Neil could've done was tell me he was moving. We'd been best friends, hadn't we?

I let myself into the house and called for Chowder before remembering that she was no longer there. I hated imagining what could've happened to her—had she been run over or...or what? She'd always come home before. I dropped my homework on the kitchen table and rubbed the dents they'd made in my arms from carrying them all the way home. That was another thing. I'd looked everywhere on the first morning before school but my knapsack had disappeared. So had my MP3 player, my jacket and my journal. I'd told my mom I was sure we'd been robbed, but she'd just raised her eyes as well as her glass of rum and asked, "Who'd want to steal that stuff?"

A note, held by a magnet, hung on the fridge and I tore it away, sending the magnet scooting across the floor and under the table. Mom had gone off for a night of bingo. I could imagine her with her thick, pink dabber and package of cigarettes, enjoying what she considered a fine night out. I sighed, crunching the paper in my fist before tossing it into the garbage. Getting down on my hands and knees, I scooped up the magnet and stuck it back where it belonged. I stared at the words printed on it and a tingle ran along my arms—*Need an Insurance Agent? Look no further than Trimbles.* I smiled. It was just a magnet.

I wandered out to the yard and lay on the hammock, dangling my leg over the side to swing it back and forth. Never before had I felt so restless. Every time I turned a corner, I expected to find something, though I didn't know what. The first week of school had been torture—even more than usual. What was going on? Mom would blame it on hormones or something, but it was more than a mood swing; there was a battle raging inside of me that I couldn't escape.

I pretended to be asleep when I heard my mother come home, but sleep was something that seemed more a memory than a reality. My once comfortable bed felt small and lumpy, and I could no longer sleep with the blind drawn—I needed to see the light from the moon and stars. I was terrified that I might be going nuts. I stared through the window, listening to the gusts of early autumn winds until, at last, I felt a wave of exhaustion roll over me and I closed my eyes.

*I tugged on the door but it refused to open. Bending and peering through the keyhole, I gazed at the forest beyond where trees crowded together with snake-like vines wrapped around their trunks. Someone stepped out and started to speak.*

"Mid pleasure and palaces though we may roam, be it ever so humble, there's no place like home."

I sat up, gasping.

"Rad!"

I scrambled out of bed, tripping over the clothes I'd left lying on the floor, and ran to the dark window. I turned then sped to the door and stopped. I had to think. Think about the dream. No, not a dream, it was real. Rad. I had to get to Rad. I had to get to Aten.

The key. I reached up to my neck but there was nothing there. I'd lost the necklace; I'd lost everything. How was I going to get back? Enrial. She'd sent me home and made me forget. I slapped my forehead. Neil!

I paced alongside my bed panting as though I'd just run a marathon. There had to be a way back, there just had to be. I plopped down on the bed and massaged my temples. Without the necklace or Neil, I couldn't return.

I wouldn't accept that. Gathering my clothes from the floor, I began to dress.

Except for the creaking swings pushed by the wind, the playground was silent and empty. There were no stars peeping through the clouds and only a shadow of the moon allowed me to see the bench. It was here that Enrial had first visited me. I would try to do anything she wanted, as long as I could go back.

"Did you hear me, Enrial? I promise I'll try." My voice sounded much more confident than I felt. I sat on the bench and crossed my arms over my chest. I'd wait here until the destruction of Earth actually happened. I'd wait forever.

The bench creaked, and I knew it was Enrial without looking over.

"That was a mean thing you did." I turned my head toward her. "I can't promise that I'll succeed, but I will try."

"There's no rush," Enrial said.

"Then why did you make it seem like I'd run out of time?"

"I had to make you realize how serious your role on Aten is. You've been running every direction without getting anywhere." She smiled at me. "I'll give you time to find what you've lost and get settled on Aten. You need to establish a safe haven for yourself—somewhere you can always be secure. Though you'd be protected in the archive, you can't perform your other duties from inside. You will need to find the Nera's children."

"How long do I have?"

"Three of your years."

"How can you possibly know that?"

"Do you think we can only look back at time in your world?" She shook her head so delicately it might have been made out of porcelain. "Now, where is it that you want to go?"

"You'll take me? Can you take me to Rad?"

"I've no idea where he is."

"Then, please, take me back to where I left Neil." I stood and touched her arm. "Why do you care so much about what happens to us?"

"We care about all our children." She covered my hand with her own.

A brilliant light flashed and I stood alone, shivering in my damp clothes at the side of the pond.

"We'd better get some rest," Neil said.

"Oh, Neil!" I ran to him. "You'll never believe what happened."

# Chapter Seventeen

"Well, there's no cottage there now." Neil returned to where I sat hugging my knees by the fire. "And there's no pond."

"She was here. Really." I stretched my hands toward the fire and let the flames warm my fingertips. Although I'd told Neil about my return home, I'd not mentioned the fact that his mom had the house up for sale. I wasn't even sure that part was real or simply an illusion like the cottage. I pointed to the water, its surface now lit by the fire's flames. "And the pond is right there."

"There's no water," Neil said.

"How can you not see it?" I got up, stomped to the edge and splashed the water with my hand. "It's right here."

"Okay, you see water and I don't. You saw a cottage, but it's not there now. It's just another Aten moment; one of those things that can't be explained."

"You seem to accept it pretty easily." I walked up to him and shook my wet fingertips at him. He flinched as the water touched his face. "See?"

"I've seen loads more weird stuff while I've been here." Neil paused. "What did it feel like, being back home?"

I pulled my gaze from the pond, trying to convince myself I wasn't going crazy. If I didn't look at it, maybe it would go away.

Neil was right—there were lots of strange things on Aten and this was merely another one to add to a growing list.

"I knew something was wrong the whole time I was back home, but I wasn't sure what. One thing is for sure, I'm glad I didn't have to stay."

"Why?"

"I had Mr. Langley for math." I laughed. "I'd rather spend time with the Hachi."

The next morning we packed up the horse and continued along the narrow trail, glad to be away from the place I thought of as the Illusion Pass. It wasn't long before we reached the end and stepped onto the sunlit meadow. The forest was far across from us, a slab of rusty colors across the horizon. Neil mounted his horse, but when I extended my arm toward him, he shook his head.

"It would be better if I checked out what's happening at the archive alone."

"You can't leave me here," I glanced at the never-ending meadow that unrolled on either side of us, "in the middle of nowhere."

"And if you come with me and Arax or the Major is there? They'd force you to open the archive."

It made sense, but I didn't like being abandoned.

"How long will you be? What if something happens to you?"

"Don't worry, I'll be back in an hour or two." He grinned. "Stay out of trouble."

I watched until the long grasses of the meadow erased both Neil and his horse and then sat down on a rock, its surface not yet warmed by the sun. What if something did happen to him? What if Rad was there and needed me? It had been three days since I'd last seen him and anything could've happened in that time. I rose up and swiped the dust from the back of my pants just as the clouds moved over the sun.

The rain started as a fine mist, coating the grass, rocks and me with a thin, wet layer. My hair curled even more around my shoulders and face as it soaked up the moisture from the air. Within minutes, the downpour came—the kind I always wanted to play in when I was a kid, but Mom never let me, claiming I might get pneumonia or something. Those were the days when she'd actually cared enough to look after me.

Neil hadn't left me any water, so I turned my face skyward and stuck out my tongue. The rain hit my eyes, forehead and cheeks, but managed to miss my mouth completely. I opened my mouth wide, wanting a drink all the more because I knew I couldn't have one.

As quickly as it had come, the rain stopped and the sun chased the mist away. The only evidence of the downpour was my wet clothes that allowed the autumn winds to bite through. No water, no jacket and no food. As far as I was concerned, Neil's plan was failing miserably.

The archive was located underground. An elevator, at the end of a narrow passage in the rocky hill, was the only way in and my charm was the key to the elevator. I'd only had a quick look inside the archive once before—filled with equipment that looked like computer terminals, shelves of books, art and who knew what else, the room was as large as a football field. Hundreds of storage units might have held anything from medical supplies to weapons and it was frustrating not knowing what kind of havoc the Major or Arax would create should either of them gain entry.

I reached an outcrop of rocks and peered around it. Off in the distance, three horses poked their noses into the grass. One of them belonged to Neil, another to Rad. I didn't recognize the third horse, but it was white like all the Danis' horses, so it may have been Catta's. They must be in the cave. I scanned the forest that was now only a few hundred meters across from me, but if anyone was there, the swaying branches would easily conceal them. I rubbed my twitching fingers against my pants. Go in or stay put?

If I simply appeared, I might be killed or forced to open the archive. Neil's plan may have been crap, but mine was no better. As soon as I walked around the bend, I'd be in full view. I gazed at the forest on the far side and noticed something snaking through the grass toward me.

I slid around the rocks that dotted the bottom of the Jagger Hills, away from whatever approached. If it was a snake, it was huge. I stamped my foot and hissed, hoping to scare it away, but the dark shape continued to slither along a path that would lead right to me.

My throat dried and my tongue seemed glued to the roof of my mouth. I pushed away and ran back the way I'd come, not caring if anyone saw me. I glanced behind me where the grass continued to part like someone running an invisible lawn mower through it. A scream vibrated from my gut and I opened my mouth to let it out just as two ears pricked through the grass. Familiar ears. Two familiar eyes followed.

"Chowder!" I crumpled to the ground and stretched out my hand.

How did she always manage to turn up just when I needed her? She sauntered over and nuzzled my fingers. Her fur was still matted and I longed to brush out the clumps that dotted her neck and sides. I gave her a hug before edging back around the bend.

The horses had strayed to the center of the meadow, but no one ventured from the cave. What could they be doing in there? I ran my tongue over my dry lips. I could get a better view of the entrance from the forest.

"Okay, Chowder, let's go."

I bent low and sprinted toward the forest. Halfway across, I realized Chowder wasn't following me and diving into the grass, I rolled and searched for her. She sat on the rocks, licking her tail. I couldn't imagine why I was putting my faith in a cat, but firmly believed she meant for me to stay by the hills. Copying Chowder's earlier movements, I crawled back to her.

"What're you trying to tell me? Not to go to the forest? Where's Rad?" This was nuts, trying to communicate with my cat, yet she seemed to know more about what was going on than I did.

Chowder balanced on the rock then soared over my head to the ground. Again, she slunk low and slithered around the bend, never looking back at me. I followed her, trying to creep lower than the grass and hoping the Awes' clothing helped me blend in with the surroundings.

Although it had recently rained only a few kilometers back, the ground here was dry and I was sure a beacon of dust followed my trek through the meadow that led into the archive. I could only hope no one watched my progress. My elbows ached as I dragged my body along and I chanced a glance ahead. Still a picture of peace—horses against a rainbow of autumn leaves, but I was almost there. I kept close to the rocky hill, stopping every few seconds to locate Chowder and get my bearings, but mostly to pluck up my nerve. Thinking Rad was inside helped, but deep down I sensed he wasn't. If that were the case, what was his horse doing here? My only hope was my cat, but instead of going toward the archive, she joined the horses grazing in the middle of the meadow. I glared at her, but Chowder simply wove around the horse's legs while they ignored her.

I'd finally made it to the archive and there was no way I could leave without trying to get my necklace back. I stood and squirmed through the narrow opening. The walls embraced me and smothered the sound of the wind in the grass. I turned sideways, creeping along the passage and every few steps, I'd stop and listen. Halfway to the elevator, flickering lights and muffled voices filtered from ahead. I held my breath and edged forward.

Arax's back was toward me, but torchlight glinted on the long, thin saber he waved in his hand. In front of him, Catta and Neil stood against the closed elevator. Neil pretended not to see me, but Catta stared at me, her eyes almost popping out of her head. Arax whirled around, keeping the saber pointed at the others. He grabbed my sleeve and threw me across the small cavern.

"Ah, Jodi. Finally our little party is complete." Arax glanced at Neil. "And you claimed to have no idea where she was. Not nice to lie to your partner."

The scene made no sense, but Arax's words were beyond reason. Partner? Arax grinned and jiggled the saber at me, the swaying necklace dangling from his wrist.

I ignored Neil because if I looked at him, I'd have to admit he'd betrayed me. I kept my gaze on the glint of the blade, but it was flashes of childhood memories I saw and Neil was the highlight of each one. What evil on Aten could steal away the dear friend Neil had once been?

Arax reached into a bundle at his feet and threw a length of rope at me. "Tie him up."

I wrapped the rope around Neil's wrists.

"Tighter." Arax peered over my shoulder, his breath sending shivers down my back. "That's better."

I knotted the rope, refusing to look into Neil's eyes, and stepped away.

"I always had a soft spot for you, Catta." Arax dismissed her with a wave of his hand before turning and pointing the blade at Neil. "But I've never had a soft spot for you."

Neil and I used to play a game when we were little. I'd lay my palms under his then try to slap his hands before he pulled them away. We believed this improved our reflexes and quick thinking skills.

"You can't kill him," I said. "I may be the only one who can get you into the archive, but he's the only one who knows how to use it."

Arax lowered the saber, hitched up his pants and glanced first at Neil then me.

"I don't believe you." He raised the weapon once again, pointing it directly at Neil's chest.

# Chapter Eighteen

My usefulness was the only thing that had ever stopped Arax from killing me, but it had never stopped him from hurting me. I imagined him writhing in pain. Pain from what? My mind raced. Ah yes, pain from the worst kind of stomachache.

I heard the clang of the saber and looked down. Arax lay on the floor, groaning and clutching his stomach. Vomit pooled around his head.

The light that had been dimly lit in Holo now flooded my brain with its brilliance. In the market, I'd wanted to push the face of the customer into the hot grill just as badly as I wanted Arax to suffer. And it had happened. I could bring people back to life, but I could also injure them simply by imagining it in my head. If this was the weakness Enrial had spoken of, then it was a weakness I could live with.

"What the hell?" Neil's eyes were wide.

I staggered over to Arax with only one thing in mind—my necklace. His eyes were closed and he seemed oblivious to me. Grasping the chain, I unwound it from his wrist then sat back on my heels and closed my fist around the charm, drawing cool comfort from the silver snake. It had taken me a week, but I'd finally retrieved it. I slipped it over my head.

"Jodi, untie me." Neil held up his hands and moved toward me.

I leaned forward, grabbed the saber from the ground and turned to him.

"Why, Neil? Why did you do it?" I didn't wait for him to answer and kept the weapon aimed in his general direction as I looked over at Catta.

"Have you seen Rad, Aladar's brother?" I asked. "He looks just like him."

Catta nodded.

"Where?"

"Jodi," Neil said. "Please."

I swung around.

"Don't. Please, don't." A salty tear slipped down my cheek and into my mouth.

"In the forest," Catta whispered.

"Where in the forest?"

"The Hachi." Her voice became stronger. "Arax ambushed and killed him. He left the body on the road that passes through their forest."

I glared at Neil when I heard him creeping toward me. He stopped and backed away.

When was this?"

"Last night," Catta said.

"I've got to go." I handed her the saber. "Will you be okay here with them?"

I didn't wait for her to answer and fled down the passage. Neil called my name, but I tuned him out as I tried to deal with the fact that more than Neil's voice and appearance had changed since I'd last been here. I ran to where Chowder waited by the horses.

"That's why you wanted me to follow you." I climbed onto Rad's horse.

Chowder crouched, wiggled her butt then shot up in front of me. She turned in a circle a few times then assumed a sphinx-like pose. I clicked my tongue, shook the reins and we were off.

Catta had said Rad was dead, but I wasn't willing to believe that. The archive was at least four hours away from the Hachi's web-covered forest and the sun was already sliding down the western sky. If my inability to rouse Paul from death had been because time had run out, then time was just about up for Rad.

I burrowed my heels into the horse. The wind whipped past my ears and lifted the hair away from my neck and, despite the cold, my skin was bathed in sweat. By the time the sun touched the horizon, I spied the trees laced with the Hachi's webs.

Without the sun sparkling on them, the webs hung oily and gray. I yanked on the reins when I neared the wide path that invited unwary travelers straight into the clutches of the over-grown spiders. When Neil and I had ventured in, the terrifying tapping of their beaks had reminded me of a hundred tiny fingers tapping on a tabletop. This time, I knew better.

Before we'd even come to a complete stop, Chowder jumped down and slunk into the meadow, the shadow of her tail flicking back and forth above the grass. I slid down the horse's side, grip-ping the reins so tightly I could feel the dent in my palm when I finally let go. I tore through the saddlebags, tossing things to the ground until I found Rad's lamp and a strange box of flint I'd seen him use to light it. My hands shook and the box tumbled to the ground, scattering the contents. I bit my lip, trying to hold back screams of anguish.

I glanced over my shoulder at the sun as it gave one last wink before disappearing. Ready to give up and journey into the for-est without the lamp, I struck a flint across the box one last time. It sparked and I held it close to the wick, the flame bouncing madly in my trembling hands. I stood, lifted the lamp and waved it from side-to-side in front of me, the grass crunching under my feet as I approached the forest. Beneath the web-cov-ered branches of the first tree, I stopped, unsure I had the nerve to go forward.

The lamp shook in my hand and after setting it on the ground, I slid down beside it, never taking my gaze from the tunnel-like path. I couldn't do it. The minute I stepped into the forest, the Hachi would be on me, sliming me with their green goo and wrapping me up in their sticky webs.

The video in my head turned on, splashing a picture of Rad's face, so sure of himself, as he cleaned his nails with my knife. I could hear the laughter in his voice after I'd slipped down the embankment in the Caves. But it was the look in his eyes when we held Chowder between us that I recalled best. He would never have abandoned me. And what had he written on the fortune-teller's card? *Archive love R.* I grabbed the lamp, jumped up and strode into the darkness of the Hachi's domain.

The web-draped trees silenced the wind and I reeled back from the smell of rotting that filled the air. My lamp cast a warm glow around me, but did little to light the path ahead. The tapping surrounded me almost as though the spiders were clapping their hands in anticipation of the feast I'd provide. I squinted, searching along the path for any sign of Rad. A shadow flitted overhead.

I ran, swinging the lamp from one side to the other. The Hachi could've wrapped up and stuffed Rad anywhere. How could I hope to find him in the dark? Another murky shape dodged alongside me.

Something thumped behind me and I twirled around—a web stretched over the path, but even worse, one of the basketball-sized Hachi streaked nimbly across it. Trailing a glistening thread behind its black body, the spider jumped to the ground. Backing away from the approaching nightmare, I stumbled and fell.

And there was Rad. The Hachi hadn't spun him up in their mummy-like cocoon and I caressed his pale face. No tingling, no warmth. I slid my hand into his, trying to ignore the glacial iciness that emanated from him while I searched my heart for the power to bring him back.

I'd almost forgotten about the Hachi and looked over my shoulder. Ten of the horrid creatures advanced, their fur-covered forelegs dancing in the air, reaching out. I envisioned them fighting amongst themselves, pecking one another with their sharp, tapping beaks. They would draw blood in their frenzy to kill each other off.

My hand fell away from Rad's and I could barely hold my head up as I watched the Hachi attack one another. Each time another spider stepped closer to us, I focused until it too joined the fray, but concentrating on them sucked all my energy; energy I needed to devote to Rad. My ability to cause injury was not only a weakness; it also made me weak. I couldn't keep it up.

I rested my head on Rad's cold chest and placed my hand over his own. I'd promised Rad I wouldn't let him slip into the darkness he'd foreseen and I'd let him down.

"I'm so sorry, Rad." I closed my eyes.

# Chapter Nineteen

Death crowded me with hazy visions and sensations—tiny dots of light played over me as I levitated and warm hands caressed my shoulders before a noose fluttered down around my neck. I tried to scream, but as in most dreams, it got tangled in my throat.

I sat up and wiped my eyes. A warm wind rustled across the sunlit meadow, bending the long shafts of dried grass as the sun drifted toward the horizon in the western sky. I stared at the rocky hills on the far side, trying to make sense of where I was and where I had been.

The Hachi! I jerked around. The path into the forest was only a few meters away, but I was on the meadow side. And so was Rad. His feet pointed toward the forest and his arms stretched over his head as though someone had dragged him by his wrists before depositing him there. I crawled to him and stared down at his pale face.

My hand shook, hovering over his chest. I was afraid to touch him, imagining him bolting upright like some zombie rising from the grave. I swallowed the fear in my throat, lowered my hand and an electrical shock ran up my arm. Leaning back, gasping, I could hardly believe Rad was alive.

"I didn't know if you'd ever wake up."

I whipped around as Catta dumped an armful of twigs on the ground, slapped her hands together and sent a sprinkling of dirt showering down. I patted my chest, making sure the necklace was still there. It was.

"Did you carry us out of the forest?"

"No, it must've been Neil." She bent, picked up a length of rope and tossed it at me. "I found this on top of you. That's the rope you'd tied him up with."

"How did he get here?"

"He got away from me last night. It's a good thing he did or you'd have been the Hachi's next meal," Catta said. "I followed him, but he was gone by the time I got here."

Some of the old Neil still existed. Could I ever forgive him? I'd have to climb that mountain when I came to it. My head jerked up.

"What about Arax?"

"Still lying on the ground when I left. It seemed an odd time to become ill." She paused, gazing at me a few moments before finally turning to Rad. "I guess Arax didn't kill him after all."

"I guess not."

He looked so different with his eyes closed; so young. Reaching over, I lifted his hands and placed them by his sides. A horse snorted and I looked up. Catta pulled a sack from her saddle and plopped it beside the twigs. She came over and stared down at Rad.

"He's just as handsome as Aladar, isn't he?" she said. "Neil may've been too late to save him, so don't get your hopes up."

"He wasn't too late." My voice was angrier than I'd meant it to be. "He'll be all right. What I can't understand is why the Hachi hadn't wrapped him up in their web."

"If he was dead then they wouldn't bother. But he wasn't dead," she narrowed her eyes and scanned my face, "was he?"

"They must've thought he was." I stood up and stretched. "What are you going to do now?"

"My plans haven't changed." She placed her hands on her hips. "I'm going to Holo to free Caden."

"That's my plan as well." I faced her. "First, I'll have to figure out where he is because he's not in Holo."

"I won't need any help finding him." She lifted the sack and strode back to her horse. "I especially won't be needing any help from you."

"So you're going to leave us here just like you left me to die in the Drylands?"

Catta stopped, her foot in one of the stirrups and the reins in her hand. After a moment, her shoulders slumped and she turned to me.

"What I did was wrong, but I was angry. Everything changed after you came that first time." Her voice was bitter. "Everything."

"In the end, it was you he married," I said.

"Oh, you may as well know the truth—he hasn't married me. Yet. But we're as good as married." Catta stuck out her arm and pointed to a silver bracelet circling her wrist. "Caden promised to marry me and he never goes back on a promise. He wasn't meant for you, do you understand?"

"No, you'd better understand." I slapped her hand away. "He's in love with me and I'm—." I hesitated.

A groan sounded behind me and I ran to Rad. His face was bathed in sweat. I dabbed at it with the bottom of my shirt. Catta bent over us, a leather flask in her hand.

"See if you can get him to drink some water."

I forced the flask between his lips and poured. The water ran over his chin and cheeks, but I was sure some went down his throat. I handed back the flask and held one of Rad's hands in my own as he moved his head from side to side, mumbling words that made no sense.

Catta plodded over to the pile of twigs, started a fire and, soon, was stirring a steaming pot over the flames. We didn't speak again except for a word here and there while we gathered more twigs from the forest's edge and got our bedding ready for the night. Though I didn't want to leave Rad's side, as darkness fell, I knew I needed to sleep. I slipped between the warm animal skins with Chowder and watched Catta nestle beside Rad.

I tore my gaze away from them and watched the fire dapple the dark grass with its playful lights. I wanted to tell her to wake me when Rad became conscious, but the emotional and physical turmoil of the last few days pulled me deep into sleep before I could say a word.

\* \* \* \*

Laughter. It seemed so out of place. I lay with my eyes closed, and waited for it to subside. A low, teasing voice then a girlish giggle. My stomach tightened and I sat up, squinting in the bright sun. Rad and Catta lounged on the other side of the dying fire, sharing a bowl of something. He lifted it to his mouth, gulped down some of the contents then passed it to her. I coughed.

"Jodi." Rad bounded up from the ground and came toward me. "About time you woke up."

"Me?"

"We've been waiting since sunup." He winked in Catta's direction.

"How are you feeling?" I asked.

"Thanks to Catta's curative powers, I feel as if I've been given renewed life."

I squashed my lips together and curled my hands into tight, little balls and try as I might, I couldn't straighten them.

Catta sauntered over and placing her hand on his arm said, "I can't take all the credit. Your own power to self-heal is great."

"Stop it!" I rose up and pushed past them. Gazing beyond the meadow, at the Jagger Hills, I flexed my fingers before turning back to them.

"What's going on here? I went in there," I pointed into the web-covered forest, "and found you. The next thing I know, you and Catta are chuckling it up and patting each other on the back."

Rad's gray eyes narrowed and fine creases sprang up between them.

"It was Neil who saved you both from the Hachi," Catta said.

"It was Neil who brought us out." I dragged my fingers through my dirty hair and forced myself to look at Rad. "But just who do you think...who do you think held your hand?"

I walked away, kicking at the ground, until I stood in the middle of the sunny meadow. Dry grass crunched behind me.

"Jodi." Rad put his hand on my shoulder and turned me around.

I stared into his eyes. Strong, unwavering and so sure of himself. He pulled me against his chest and my body tingled from the contact. I shut down my whirling thoughts and let the moment wrap its safety net around me.

"I know what you did and I will never be able to repay you that debt. No one has ever steered one of my visions from its course, but I knew if anyone could do it, you could. I saw darkness and you brought me light." He leaned back and grinned. "This ability of yours, it's not something we should let Catta or the rest of the world know about, is it?"

"I feel like an idiot." I swiped my hand over my wet cheeks. "So many things have happened and then you and Catta...it was too much."

"Tell me what happened." Rad gestured to the ground and we sat, facing one another.

I poured out the events of the last few days—how Juna had helped me escape from Holo; how Neil had helped me escape the Nera; discovering Paul's body and my inability to revive him; finding Arax and Catta by the archive; and, finally, Neil's betrayal.

"He was my best friend."

"And he fell into Aten's trap. It happens."

"When I heard you'd been dead since the night before, I wasn't sure I could get to you in time. I'd promised I would."

"And you did." He tapped his finger against his lips. "Catta said that the minute you came into the cave, Arax suddenly succumbed to illness. What do you think happened there?"

"I'm not sure."

"Yet I think I can guess," Rad said.

"Enrial warned me I had a weakness. Depending on how you look at it, injuring people might be considered one." I stared at the toes of my boots. "I don't want to hurt anybody, but I couldn't let Arax kill Neil."

"There seems to be a downside to all abilities," Rad's voice was bitter. "You've just experienced it for the first time and now you're going to have to learn how to use the ability wisely, if at all."

I was afraid to tell him that it was my ability that burned the man's face in Holo's market. What would he think of me then?

"Why did Enrial give me this power? What good does she believe I can do with it?"

He stood and drew me gently up. "I think we'd better pay a visit to Nereen and see if Nashira can tell us exactly what Enrial has planned for Aten."

# Chapter Twenty

The sun wasn't strong enough to warm the breeze whispering across the meadow. I stared over my shoulder at Catta's retreating figure as she rode toward Ganodu and when I could no longer see the flicking of her horse's tail, I shifted on our own horse and faced forward.

"Do you think she's really going back to Ganodu?" I'd finally been able to convince Catta that Caden wasn't in Holo. She claimed she'd return home, but I wasn't so sure.

"Are you afraid she'll find Caden before you do?"

"What would it matter if she did?" Knowing Catta, she'd drag Caden off to be married, conveniently forgetting to tell him I'd returned to Aten.

"I'd think it mattered a great deal. After all, wasn't Caden one of the reasons you came back?"

"Was he? I don't remember." Why had I returned? Caden? Neil? To save the world? "I don't know if it's such a good idea going to Nereen. They want to lock me up."

"I imagine they haven't the power to do that."

The horse bent its head and snatched at one of the few bits of green grass dotting our path. Rad tugged on the reins, but not before the beast had snagged a decent-sized mouthful.

"And," Rad continued, "you're running out of options. It isn't safe to return to Holo or the archive, as I'm sure the Major will have both points covered. If you want answers, then Nereen is a good place to start."

Rad and I had argued that morning before we'd left the edge of the Hachi forest. Having retrieved the real necklace from Arax, I'd wanted to go back to the archive, get inside and explore, but he hadn't budged. I knew I could have gone back by myself—I simply had to envision the elevator in my head, hold the charm and I would be there in seconds. Yet the thought of using the charm to travel around Aten unnerved me. What if I ended up somewhere else altogether?

I fondled the necklace then tucked it under my shirt. I didn't want to take the chance of being whisked off the back of Rad's horse and landing in the middle of nowhere simply because the thought was in my head. My hand fell to Chowder, curled up into a fluffy ball between Rad and me. Her purring throbbed against my fingertips.

"How long till we get there?" I asked.

"Two days, maybe three. Depends on what we run into." The tightness in his voice sent a shudder through my gut.

The late afternoon sky was the color of pearls and cast a pink glow on the world around us, both promising and foreboding. Winter would be here soon and even though the Awes' clothing provided some warmth, they could never protect me from the bitter cold. I'd nodded off several times during the day and, once, nearly fallen from the horse only to be yanked back by Rad. I'd thought it hilarious, but he'd only given me a token smile. Something was on his mind and as we crested a small rise, I realized what it must have been.

Five truck-sized boulders erupted from the earth—the Phosphor Caves. Our horse seemed to sense the significance of the moment as it stopped at the top of the rise and turned, allowing us a full view of the rocks below. Rad hadn't mentioned Stala's name since we'd jumped into the cold, black pool to escape the Kurage. Although she'd been on my mind, I'd been afraid to talk about her, hoping Rad might be able to forget.

"We'll camp here." He slid down the side of the horse, walked to the nearest boulder and ran his palm over its rough surface.

I swallowed, suddenly thirsty. "Are we going in?"

"I am, tomorrow. You'll stay here with the horse." Rad looked at me, but I don't think he saw me at all. "If I'm not out by nightfall, continue south until you reach the forest."

"I'll come with you." Could he hear the fear in my voice?

"I'll think about it."

I crawled out of my bedding when the sound of Rad's moans filled the air, and grasped his shoulder. His eyes fluttered, then opened.

"What is it?" His voice was strong even though he'd just woken up. He reached out and used the small box of flints to light the lamp beside him.

"You're having a nightmare." The cold night wrapped around me and I brushed my hands up and down my arms.

He rose and led me back to my own bedding, watching as I slipped under the covers, easing my legs around the warm spot where Chowder slept. Rad paced beside me then, with a sigh, sat down on his heels.

"I suppose you deserve to know the truth." Rad swallowed and I waited for him to go on. "Soon after my sixteenth celebration, my father planned an excursion to Atoll, a town many days' travel from Windore. Before he left, I had a vision of the future, clear and terrifying—he would die on that trip. I knew it, but didn't say anything to him because there was nothing we could do to stop it."

"Then why do you feel so much guilt? You're not responsible."

"I've always wondered if the future I see is of my own making. Perhaps if I didn't have the vision, it wouldn't happen." He stood, his body a black smudge against the half moon. "I couldn't stay in Windore, always knowing who would die."

"What did Aladar say?"

"Aladar?" Rad's laughter was hollow. "Aladar's belief in me never wavered. He's my main reason for leaving—I didn't think I could endure knowing anything unfortunate would happen to my brother." Rad wandered back to his bedding and lay down, his silhouette disappearing from sight.

My heart ached for Rad, but I hadn't the words to comfort him. I hugged my arms across my chest and wondered for the hundredth time if Aten held the promise of anything other than misery. And what would happen to me? Rad would find comfort with Stala after he'd rescued her; Neil would continue to hide from his own demons; and Caden? Catta said Caden had promised to marry her and he'd never go back on a promise. That didn't leave much for me.

\* \* \* \*

Why are nights so deadly quiet that even the sound of a scampering beetle can be heard? The mornings are the complete opposite—noisy and full of life. I rubbed my eyes and sat up.

Our horse drank water from the pool on the far side of the previous night's fire. No warmth radiated from the fire now, just a few speckles of ash lifted by the slight breeze. I didn't need to call—I knew Rad had gone into the caves without me. I snuggled down into the bedding, afraid that, if I got up, I'd have to do something. I'd have to go in after him.

Chowder brushed up against me, clumps of fur hanging like Christmas decorations from her coat. I imagined my hair didn't look much better. I patted her before noticing a dead mouse beside me on the grass.

"I'm hungry, Chowder, but not that hungry."

I hauled over one of the bags and rummaged around for a bit of food, discovering there wasn't much left. I stared at the boulders. Large and menacing as they were, they were the smallest hurdle to finding Rad and Stala. I squirmed out from under the covers.

"You stay here. I won't be long." Who was I trying to convince, Chowder or myself?

The small niches in the rock were hard to navigate on my own and by the time I reached the top, my fingers were scraped and my toes cramped. I flung myself over the edge then lay, panting, on my back. The sky was filled with gray clouds, sharp around their edges. I counted to five, trying to regain my strength then got up and stumbled to the hole that led into the Kurage's underground home. The humid air wafted from below, a startling contrast to the outside world. I grasped the slimy rope and lowered myself into the narrow shaft. Working my way like an upside-down crab, I felt as though everyone else in the world had left.

This time I was ready for the drop onto the floor and, extending my legs, landed on my feet. Even without my flashlight, the green walls were immediately visible and using their meager light to guide me, I tiptoed across the small cavern to the fissure in the far wall. Sure this was the way we'd gone before, I slipped through the crack.

I stayed close to the wet walls, letting their rough surface scratch my arm. Soon the chirping started, comforting in a way because it meant I was going in the right direction. The acrid smell of bat guano hit me like a slamming door. How could anyone live with that?

Slinking along the narrow path, I prayed I wouldn't take another trip down the slope. What was I doing here? How could I hope to help? There was a chance Rad and Stala would escape and I'd be left behind. I stopped abruptly, scattering stones over the side. What an idiot! I had my necklace and could leave anytime I wanted. Not only that, I had the power Enrial had warned me about—I could hurt anyone who tried to stop me. I grinned and sped along the narrow ledge, not caring that the bats had taken flight.

After a lifetime surrounded by the eerie green light, I was thirsty, hungry and lost in the Phosphor Caves. I'd tripped through so many caverns and tunnels I might have made it all the way to Holo underground, while Rad and Stala may have already returned to the campsite. I stopped to catch my breath and wiped a film of sweat from my forehead. I should've stayed outside because I'd never find them here. Now was my chance to try the charm. If I envisioned Chowder, the horse and the five boulders, would the charm take me there? I reached under my damp shirt. The necklace stuck to my sweaty skin like a suction cup and when I tugged, it came away with a pop. I bit my lip and focused on a spot just above my head. Chowder. The horse. The five...

Enraged voices rang out. I dropped the necklace and whipped around, angling my head to the sounds of slashing steel on rock—they were coming from the tunnel beside me. I ran toward the noise, my fists pumping at my sides and the green walls beckoning like flashing pedestrian lights. I splashed through a small stream, broke through an opening and skid to a halt. My boots slid along the mossy path and I fell forward, onto my knees. The source of the noise was only meters away.

# Chapter Twenty-One

Seven of the Kurage held spears, jabbing them at Rad and Stala's chests and forcing their backs against the wall. Perhaps because of Stala's angry cries, they didn't hear me.

"We don't belong here. Why don't you listen to me? You've never listened!" She tried to shove the spear aside.

"What would happen if everyone decided it was all right to leave? What would happen to the Kurage then?" The speaker drove his spear into Stala's arm. "No, you're staying here."

Blood trickled down, but Stala didn't even flinch, she merely lifted her head and stared at the man.

"Then I beg you to kill me, for this is not life." She glanced at Rad. "But you must set my friend free."

Rad struggled, flinging himself against the spears, getting a few deep cuts for his trouble.

"Let them go." My voice wobbled as much as my legs.

The Kurage twisted around, their mouths gaping open. Rad slammed together the heads of two Kurage and they dropped to the ground. Stala kicked the knees of her tormentor then pulled the spear from her arm, and drawing it back, jammed the butt end into someone else. Four down, three to go.

Rad wrestled with one on the cave floor while another bounced nearby, jabbing his spear, obviously afraid he might spike his companion by mistake. I focused on the Kurage above Rad, my energy draining, and when I looked, the man was lying crumpled and moaning on the moss. Rad continued to fight the man on top of him, his hands sliding along the Kurage's arms. I turned to Stala.

Her back was pressed against the wall, a Kurage's fingers circling her neck. I clapped my hands together, imagining his head between them and he dropped like a zapped mosquito. Rad stood and brushed tiny flecks of moss from his clothing, his adversary lying motionless the floor. He looked up at me.

"We were managing just fine on our own."

I attempted a smile, but I felt more like joining the Kurage on the ground than anything else.

"We'd better get out of here before the others come," Stala said.

"What about..." I gestured up and down her transparent body. "Can you leave here?"

"I'd rather die Upworld than stay another moment here," Stala said over her shoulder as she turned down a tunnel. "I thought I could handle it, but I was wrong."

Rad and I hurried after her. As we traveled along the endless paths, I hungered for a breath of fresh air. My feet no longer belonged to me, they simply kept moving, fuelled by fear.

"I have to stop," I said.

"We haven't time." Rad gripped my arm and pulled me along.

"No, I can't. You two go ahead." I bent forward and rested my hands on my knees.

"We must keep moving," Stala said impatiently. "They won't be giving us any second chances."

Breathing in the Phosphor Caves was like trying to suck air through a feather pillow. The fight with the Kurage had emptied me, as had the Hachi when I'd found Rad. Perhaps the weakness Enrial had spoken of was my lack of energy after using my ability to injure. I straightened up. Running and gasping for air was far better than thinking about power I didn't want to admit having.

"I'm okay now. I just needed to catch my breath," I said.

"Doesn't sound as if you've succeeded." Rad wrapped his arm under mine, almost carrying me. I leaned against him and the tingling sensation revived me.

"I think I can do it on my own." I pulled away from him.

Rad's arm dropped to his side and he nodded, pushing me forward. We sped through the bat-filled cave, sending stones sliding and bats soaring. It was as though we'd awakened the Phosphor Caves from a deep sleep. When we reached the fissure in the far wall, the bats had almost quieted, then something else disrupted their rest—the Kurage must have been close behind us.

The rope leading from the caves, dangled tantalizingly above our heads. Stala jumped, grasped it with both hands and disappeared into the shaft. Rad lifted me.

"Hurry."

I needed no encouragement and closed my hands around the damp rope. I began to slide. Wrapping my legs around it, I wiped one hand then the next on my pants. Using muscles I didn't even know I had, I pulled myself up. The rope tightened as Rad took hold.

The shaft walls enveloped me and for the first time, I believed we'd make it. Rad's breaths followed me, reassuring because they were so near. I heard the cries of the Kurage as they burst through the fissure and the rope suddenly swung loose below me. I glanced down, unable to see what was going on, but it was clear that Rad was no longer below me. I pushed my cramped legs and back against the walls, listening to the scuffle erupting below.

"Jodi, keep going," Rad yelled.

My mind and body turned to stone; I couldn't move. I gazed up through the passage at a darkening gray sky. No sign of Stala—she must've made it Upworld. The Kurage's angry voices slid up the shaft to my hiding spot. We'd come into their world uninvited then stolen away one of their own; they would surely kill Rad. I inched my body down the wall until the opening gaped underneath, then I let go of the rope.

I plummeted into the eerily lit green cavern. They had Rad mashed against the wall, his nose buried deep in the green moss. I ran between them, shoving aside the Kurage. Taking my appearance in stride, they simply forced my face into the earthy-smelling moss. With the last of my strength, I reached out and slipped my pinkie finger through Rad's. Sliding the fingers of my other hand around the charm, I envisioned Rad and me beside Chowder, the horse and the five boulders.

The moist air of the caves and the sounds of the Kurage disappeared, replaced by the hint of a cool evening breeze. I'd done it! Just as I'd been able to travel to Aten with Chowder, I could use the charm to transport not only myself, but also someone else while I was here. Rad staggered back and by the astonished look on his face, the improbability of what had happened struck him. He stared at me for several seconds then cocked one eyebrow.

"There's much more to you than first meets the eye."

Stala worked her way down the boulder, her feet expertly finding each tiny notch in the rock. When she turned, I could almost make out the surprised look on her face in the dusk.

"Is this some sort of joke?" she asked.

Rad sprang up and grabbed one of the animal skins from the ground and wrapped it around her transparent form. Digging into a saddlebag, he drew out a long cloth strip, which he secured around Stala's injured arm.

"We have to take you somewhere safe," he said.

"Juna should be able to help her," I said. But would she be willing to?

"Onto the horse, both of you."

The thought of sitting down and surely falling asleep as I rode was tempting. Yet sharing that small space with Stala's slippery form sickened me and, as ashamed as I was of that, I couldn't bring myself to touch her.

"Rad, I can take Stala to Nereen. We don't need to waste any time traveling by horse now that I know the charm works."

"Can you take all three of us?"

"I wasn't even sure I'd be able to do it with one person. Look, this is all new to me and I don't want to take the chance of losing someone in the middle of nowhere." I looked around the campsite and spotted Chowder watching me from my own strewn bedding. "I'll come right back for you and my cat. I'm not sure, but I should be able to take the horses, too."

"What are you talking about?" Stala said.

"Jodi appears to have the ability to travel in the same manner as the Nera's outports. She'll take you to Nereen and their healer can help get you back into Upworld shape," Rad said. "It's our only hope."

I yawned and fought to keep my eyes open. "Maybe I should rest first. I don't think I can even make it to bed, never mind Nereen. Will you be okay for a few hours, Stala?"

She nodded her head. "As long as there's no sun, I'll survive for a while."

Rad scrounged in his bags for the few remaining morsels of dried fruit and divided them between us. We drank water from the spring and I was relieved that something so clean and fresh could come from beneath those boulders. I burrowed down into my bedding and drifted in and out of sleep, occasionally hearing snatches of Rad and Stala's conversation.

"Paul?"

"Dead."

Later:

"Like a sister." Rad's voice floated from the surrounding darkness.

"Since the beginning?"

"Since the first day we met."

"I'm glad to hear it."

I tried to awaken, but even my curiosity wasn't enough to rouse me. I wanted only to curl up into a cat-like ball and sleep for the next month.

"It's time." Rad's words hung heavily in the cold morning air.

I sat up, my face feeling swollen and numb. After taking a few sips of water, I stood and tottered over to Stala.

"I'll be back," I said in my best Arnold Schwarzenegger voice. The humor was lost on them. I sighed. "Okay, let's go."

I tried not to shudder as I slipped my hand into Stala's, but discovered her shell was firm and only a bit like greasy pizza dough. I held the charm and envisioned Nereen as I remembered it—its white, triangle-shaped building and lovingly landscaped gardens. When I opened my eyes, Nereen's beauty surrounded us, yet something had changed. Instead of the Nera tending their plants, they were out in force, patrolling the invisible barrier surrounding their home and, within seconds, they converged on Stala and me.

# Chapter Twenty-Two

I was so startled it didn't even occur to me to grab hold of Stala and the charm and return to the relative safety of the campsite. Before I'd done a three-sixty of the grounds, the Nera were upon us.

"Restrain her."

My shoulders slumped and I turned. Nashira towered over me, her brows drawn close over her eyes and her anger distorting her normally beautiful features. Two Nera held my wrists.

"Take the necklace." Nashira nodded toward my chest and the chain was lifted over my head.

"Enrial gave me that necklace. If she wanted you to have it, she'd have given it to you."

"The Mother has long forsaken us, so I've decided it's time we took Aten in hand."

"What's going on here?" Stala dropped the blanket she'd wrapped over her like a cloak before we left.

"And who have we here?" Nashira circled around us. "A Kurage. Not safe to leave the shelter of your caves."

"She needs Juna's help." I followed Nashira's progress with my gaze. "Why are you doing this? I haven't come here to harm you."

"You want me to trust you, yet you slipped from the safety of Juna's net in Holo. Do you not trust us?"

Her question was too close to the truth, but I wouldn't let her know. "I had a few things to do before coming to Nereen. You see, here I am and I'm not trying to escape or hide from you."

"You left us over nine seasons ago. Where did you go? What have you been up to in that time?"

"I'm an outsider. I went back home for one day." Tears of exasperation lit my eyes. She didn't want to believe me.

Nashira leaned toward me, her lips pulled back over her teeth. Stala stepped between us.

"You'll not harm this one."

"You look familiar, but I've not run into many Kurage before." Nashira studied Stala's transparency. "Yet I know you."

"It's with Rad that Jodi and I travel."

Nashira quickly hid her surprise. She looked around, exaggerating her confusion. "I don't see him."

"I'm supposed to go back for him," I said.

"Ah, the necklace." She tapped her teeth with her long fingernail then signaled for the Nera to release me. "I remember the first night when you escaped Nereen. I always wondered how you managed to end up on the other side of our defenses."

"Nashira, you're not as evil as you are making yourself appear. Please let Juna help Stala, she'll die otherwise."

Nashira nodded to one of the Nera. "Take her to Juna."

I patted Stala's arm and whispered, "Thanks," before she was led down the hill.

"Now what do we do with you?" Nashira asked.

"I came here for help and information," I said. "I didn't come here to be robbed."

"I've only taken what is rightfully ours; I need nothing more from you. You're right, of course, I'm not the evil queen." She motioned toward the white building. "You look tired, dirty and hungry—much like the first time we met."

How long before Rad figured out I wasn't coming back? Once he did, he'd be here in a day or two. Could he help get me out of this mess? Amazing how trouble followed me wherever I went on Aten. I studied Nashira's stiff back as she led the way down the hill—would she be satisfied with the necklace or would she want more? Did she realize she would need me to open the archive? Most importantly, how could I get my necklace back?

I was in heaven. The waters of the huge tub swirled around me, floating out over a week's worth of sweat and grime. I let thoughts of Aten flow from my mind and for a moment, I allowed myself the luxury of simply being. I didn't care if the Nera had turned on the essence that would make me forget about the outside world. I wanted to forget.

Someone knocked on the door. I didn't answer, hoping they'd go away, but they knocked again.

"Yes?" My voice sounded as weak as my spirit felt.

Juna popped her head in and held up my Awes' clothing, folded and already cleaned. "I need to speak with you."

"Is it Stala? Is she all right?" I sat up, luxury forgotten.

"She'll be fine before you know it." Juna waved the subject aside. "I came to talk about you."

I squirmed down into the water. I didn't want to talk about me.

"Nashira said that you'd spoken of Enrial, The Mother. How did you know her true name?"

I stared at the jet's bubbles erupting on top of the water, hiding me from Juna's gaze. If I told her the truth, would it help me?

"She visited me when I returned to my time and said it was my job to get Aten back on track." I thrust out my chin. "And she gave me the necklace."

"But you are a child and the charm is a powerful tool."

"I'm not a child." I gestured toward the towel and she handed it to me. Getting up from the tub and wrapping the towel around me, I said, "Do you know that I've taken care of my own mother for years? Me. I was the one who cleaned and cooked and shopped. I may have messed up a few times on Aten, but I think I'm capable of doing the job Enrial sent me to do."

"She must have given you more than the charm to turn Aten around." Juna angled her head. "Did she mention anything else?"

I scrubbed my hair with a second towel, hiding my face. "No. But I can't do anything without the charm."

"It's doubtful Nashira will return it to you. She's grown tired of Aten's ways, and our own reason for being here has been eliminated. There will be no more offspring." Juna's voice sounded sad and I almost felt sorry for her.

"Why did you and the Major ever come here to begin with? Why didn't you just let humans take care of their own world?"

Her eyes widened at the mention of the Major. "So you know the truth about Tuldume? He became power hungry and turned against us."

"Why didn't you send him back to wherever it is you come from?"

"Once the last transport left, there was no going back." Juna took a deep breath. "We knew that before we came, but we never expected Enrial to abandon us without a backward glance."

"She hasn't abandoned you—I saw her a few days ago right here on Aten."

"She hasn't time for those who've outlived their usefulness."

"I don't believe that."

Yet there may have been some truth in what Juna believed— hadn't Enrial been prepared to send me home if I hadn't been willing to do what she asked? But without the necklace, I couldn't do anything.

I stood in front of the statue that had once burned my fingers when I'd touched it. Carved from some white, marble-like stone, it depicted the same snake as my charm. Arax had once called it a fertility symbol. Unlike the other tall statues lining the hall-ways, this one attracted me, though to everyone else here it was simply a cold piece of stone. Why, when I was in Nereen before, had the snake statue blistered my finger when I'd touched it?

"It was a mistake for Enrial to involve you in our world." Nashira's voice broke through my thoughts.

"This is my world." I didn't turn around.

"Until we can find a way of returning you home, you'll stay here. Then when Nereen is secure, we'll turn on the essence. That will make it easier for you," she said. "Come and share a meal with us."

I followed her along the sunlit passage to the dining hall and sat on one of the pillows surrounding the tables. If Nashira forced me to remain in Nereen, the essence they pumped in would make me forget about everything that had happened both on Aten and in my own time.

"Is that it then? You'll make me forget everything I've done and seen here?" I shook my head, bewildered. "I can't go on with my life like none of this happened."

"Oh, but you can and you will." Nashira picked up one of the steaming rolls from a tray.

"You mean you'd use your essence to make me forget?" I pushed away from the table.

"Perhaps we can even find a way to send you home," Nashira said. "I imagine you'd want to return to your family and friends. You must miss them."

Did I? Nashira was offering me the chance to leave Aten and forget everything about it. I'd return to Mom and Gramps and… Who else? Neil wouldn't be there and his whereabouts would always remain a mystery to me. Yet I'd also forget about Caden, Rad and all the other friends I'd made here. Is that what I wanted? No, Enrial had tried that already—there was nothing that could make me forget.

"I need to think about it," I said.

"Jodi, there is no thinking about it. If there is a way, you'll go back whether you like it or not." Nashira popped the food in her mouth and snapped her teeth shut.

# Chapter Twenty-Three

I paced across the deep, white carpet in my bedroom. I'd checked in on Stala as she slept, relieved to discover her body less transparent. When Rad got here, she'd be whole again and the two of them could ride off into the sunset. I picked up a small pillow from the bed and threw it against the darkened window.

The constant sight of all the Nera had reminded me of my situation, and finally I'd escaped to the room they'd assigned me. My thoughts were like a plate of spaghetti—each time I started on one strand, another thought was picked up. After a while, I almost welcomed the idea of breaking free from all my memories of Aten.

What would happen if I did leave? Everyone would go on with lives probably made easier by my absence. And the Nera would control the archive. Would that be so bad?

I stared out the window at the darkening sky. With the barrier in place, I couldn't escape from Nereen without the charm. Nashira was right, in the end it didn't matter what I wanted. If she could, she'd send me back home and there wasn't anything I could do about it.

I slid open the bedroom door and peeked down both ends of the empty hall. Assured by the barrier's presence, the Nera weren't worried about me getting away. I wasn't even sure what I hoped to find by sneaking around Nereen in the dead of night. The charm? Not likely. What then?

Pieces of the puzzle were missing and without knowing what the final picture looked like, I wasn't even sure where the pieces fit. Maybe I wouldn't have any choice about going home or staying here and being forced to forget, but I was determined to discover as much as I could before either of those things happened.

I crept close to the wall, slipping around the statues and hiding in their shadows. No one patrolled the inside of the building though I was sure Nashira had Nera guarding the exterior. They were afraid of something getting into Nereen or they wouldn't have closed in on us so quickly when we'd arrived.

Following the triangular route of the passage, I discovered most of the doors were closed and the dining hall dark; everyone was asleep. I let out the breath I'd been holding and leaned back. The snake statue stared at me from across the passage and I again wondered why it burned me and no one else. I crossed over and grazed my fingers over its surface. The heat sprang up, like tiny jets of water. Hot water. This time, I didn't draw back my hand. Instead, I slammed my palm onto the base of the snake, shutting out the pain of the scalding marble.

I don't know how long I stood there searing my hand, but finally tore away and raised it to my face. The image of a coiled snake embossed my right palm, from the top of my middle finger to my wrist. And it didn't hurt.

I wandered down the hall toward my bedroom, staring at the glistening welt. I no longer believed in coincidence—Enrial had said she could point me in the right direction. Perhaps this was part of her plan. As I neared my room, I stretched out my hand and the door slid open. The odd thing was, I hadn't even touched the surface. I closed the door, tried again and the door slid open as if by magic. I smiled. Now I had a key no one could take from me.

I crept under the white bedcovers and laid my palm on my chest, where the charm had once been. I'd been going crazy with indecision, but was now focused and sure of one thing—I wouldn't be staying in Nereen.

I slept soundly. For the first time in weeks, I looked ahead and saw only one path to choose from, instead of a multi-forked road. The next morning, I bounded out of bed and dressed into my Awes clothing, the shimmering green fabric fitting like a second skin. I'd go see Stala first.

Awake though still in bed, she glanced up from the tray set on her lap and said, "You seem in fine mood."

"I am." I shrugged. "Don't ask me why, but I've a feeling good things are going to happen."

"Nothing good ever happens on Aten." She raised a glass of creamy-colored liquid to her lips, gulped it down and grimaced. "Nothing."

"You're looking more Upworldish today." I sat on the edge of the bed and fanned my hand at the humidity in the room. "How're you feeling?"

"Juna is working wonders. Much faster than the last time I went through it."

"How did you do it the last time?"

Stala settled her back against the pillows and faced the windows. Her room looked out onto a garden filled with tall, multi-petaled, orange flowers.

"An old man, Lateer, found me in the canyon after I'd left the caves. I'd never believed what they said about Upworld and I decided to find out for myself. Of course, they were right—Upworld is deadly to the Kurage." She spread out her pink hands and turned them over and over, as though she couldn't believe they belonged to her.

"He took me to his home, a little hole in the canyon wall, but it was beautiful as far as I was concerned. He took care of me, using the waters of the Deakin River to soothe and feed my shell until, one day, I was whole." She fell silent.

"What happened to Lateer?" I asked.

"He became ill; he was old after all. We switched roles and I took care of him until he died. I left him in his small cave, the only place he'd cared about, and barricaded the entrance with rocks. No one will ever disturb him."

"I'm sorry, Stala."

"We all die," she said. "I'm only happy that when I do, it will be above ground instead of below."

I nodded, not sure what to say to that.

"What are your plans?" she asked.

"I don't know. Nashira wants to send me back to my time and take over control of the archive. I could try and get the charm back, but I've this feeling I don't really need it anymore." I rubbed the now-calloused welt against my pants. "It looks like I only need to get out of here, find Caden and free him."

"Will you wait for Rad?"

"I don't know." I chewed the side of my nail. "I think it would be best if I left as soon as possible. That is, if I can find a way out of here."

The door opened and Nashira flew into the room. A chain with a small chunk of silver swung from her hand.

"What have you done to it?"

"Done to what?" I asked.

She shoved the chain in my face. "The charm, you fool!"

I shoved her hand away and glanced at what she held. "I've done nothing to it. You've picked up the wrong chain."

"I wore it around my neck as I slept and this is what I found there this morning."

"Do you think I came and switched necklaces during the night? If that were true, Nashira, I'd be long gone by now."

She narrowed her eyes and positioned her fists on her hips, the chunk of silver twirling against her thigh.

"I don't know how you did it."

"It wasn't me." No, but it might've had something to do with the snake statue in the hallway and the welt on my hand. I'd keep that little secret to myself. Oddly enough, the demise of the charm didn't bother me. "Maybe the charm was meant to self-destruct if you took it from me."

Nashira's gaze roved across my face. Finally, she nodded and headed back to the doorway. Before she went through, she turned around. "This doesn't mean you're free to leave Nereen."

"She's got some major mood swing problems," I said as the door slid shut. "Juna should give her something for them."

Stala laughed.

"You don't laugh very often." I sat down on the bed again.

"There isn't much to laugh about, is there?"

"Why are you always so negative?" I thought of the snippets of conversation I'd heard between Rad and her as I slept. "There are lots of good things happening in your life."

"You're right." Her smile was a bit lopsided. "I'll start appreciating what I have."

"I'll let you get some rest; there's a few things I still have to do."

I headed to the dining hall for breakfast, remembering Stala's smile. I'd disliked her in the beginning, but now realized she was loyal, brave and a true friend. It was obvious she loved Rad and Rad loved her. Why, when I allowed myself to admit it, did that make me feel sick inside?

I forced myself to think about Rad as I scooped food onto my plate. I'd ignored my chaotic feelings about him ever since the first electrifying moment we'd met. Why was that? I stared at my plate, remembering all that had happened in the past week and a half, and my appetite vanished.

I loved him.

# Chapter Twenty-Four

I was supposed to love Caden. Was it possible to love two people at once? If so, why did I have to fall for two guys who were already spoken for? I scraped my uneaten meal into the garbage and piled my plate on top of the others waiting to be washed. Brushing past Nera, I stumbled through the open glass doors and into the gardens.

Even though Enrial said she couldn't control me, could she control everyone else? Funny how the first time I'd come to Aten I'd been rescued by Caden and this time, by Rad. Very convenient. I bent my neck and looked at the Caribbean blue-colored sky and rolled up my sleeves. The air was warmer than it had been for the past week. Maybe Enrial could even control the weather.

I shook my head. I was becoming paranoid beyond reason. Enrial might put things in our paths, but we commanded our own destinies. Hadn't I told Rad that very thing? If I were to do what she asked, then I'd need to get out of here. I put her out of my mind and stalked back into the building, making straight for Stala's room.

"I have to leave," I announced when the door opened. "Today."

"Where are we going?" She swung her legs over the side of the bed.

"Just me. I've got to find Caden, then hide somewhere and wait till everything dies down and people lose interest in me."

"I don't think that will happen," Stala said. "I'm sure of it."

"Could you do me a favor?" She nodded and I continued, my voice trembling. "Take care of Chowder for me, though knowing her, she'll find me somehow."

"At least wait until Rad arrives."

I bent and hugged her. "Thanks for everything."

"You shouldn't go alone." Stala struggled to rise from the bed.

"You're still weak. Please, don't worry, I'll stay as far away from trouble as I can." I backed toward the door. "Tell Rad…tell him I appreciate everything he did for me."

I turned from her room and slipped through the nearest door into the garden. I had no belongings, nothing to hold me back. Closing my eyes, I imagined the forest across from the archive, but the snake-shaped welt lacked the power to transport me as the charm had—I was still in Nereen. I was sure I'd been given the welt for a reason, if only to get through the locked door in the Nera's barrier. I started up the hill and, as I passed the garden shed, a little hiss escaped from behind it.

"Pssst."

I stopped. One of the Nera pressed her back against the small building. I'd sat beside her at dinner one night, the last time I'd been here and I searched my memory for her name—of course, Heline.

"Hello," I said.

"Keep your voice down, please." She crooked her finger. "Come here, where they can't see you."

Safely hidden from view, I waited, somewhat impatiently, for Heline to continue.

"You're looking for Caden?"

I leaned forward. "Yes, do you have any idea where he is?"

She poked her head around the corner as two women

marched by the other side of the shed. Heline waited until they were farther along before turning back to me.

"You won't find him by leaving."

"What do you mean?"

"He's right here in Nereen. He has been all along."

My mouth hung open as I tried to form the word 'what', but nothing came out. It wasn't possible that Caden was here—he'd been taken by the Major and locked away.

"It's true." Heline must've sensed my doubt. "You can search all you want outside Nereen, but you'll never find him."

"Then, where is he?" I gazed around the peaceful grounds. "Why is he hiding?"

"He isn't hiding, he's a prisoner."

"Why would you imprison Caden?" My mind somersaulted over the implications.

"I didn't imprison him. In fact, I've fought Nashira ever since he was brought here. It isn't right, I told her, to lock away your own son."

"I thought the Major had him."

"Tuldume," she wrinkled her nose as though she'd caught a whiff of a bad smell, "couldn't hold Caden long. He was afraid that once Caden mastered his ability, he could put a stop to the Major's plans. Think how easy it would be for Caden to use his voice. The Major's threats to Nereen's safety were enough to convince Nashira to become Caden's jailer—she's the only one with the power to do so."

My knees wobbled and I slid down the wall of the shed, feeling small and deflated. Nashira was arrogant, domineering and moody, but I never thought her capable of this. "Can you take me to him?"

"I'll tell you where you can find him."

I avoided Nashira for the rest of the day, eating and waiting in my room for night to fall. I stood with my ear pressed against the door until the hallway was quiet and I was sure the Nera were in bed, then tiptoed to the window and crept outside. I moved around the house and continued down the hill to an area I'd never been. Heline had said Caden was imprisoned inside a building deep within the woods. I relied on the moon for light, afraid a torch or candle would alert the Nera. Luckily, the sky was cloudless.

Birch trees filled the woods, their white bark reflecting the moonlight. I ignored the branches that scratched my arms as I followed the narrow track Heline had promised would lead me to Caden. I walked for well over ten minutes, breathing in the darkness and crisp air until I reached a sandy clearing. In its center, a small, cylindrical structure sat atop three meter-high supports.

My stomach flip-flopped. I'd wondered if the whole thing was an elaborate trick, but now sensed Caden's presence—he was inside. I ventured forward, reaching out with my palm. If there was a barrier, I was sure the snake-shaped welt would see me safely through.

I climbed a metal ladder and extended my arm, noticing it shaking in rhythm with my heart. This was what I'd traveled so far for—to find Caden and free him. I pressed my palm toward the door and it whooshed open. The air sparkled as though there were a thousand tiny fireflies inside, and Caden lay in the center, suspended a meter off the ground. I took a deep breath and stepped through the door.

His long, black lashes lay over his cheeks and had there been a bed under him, anyone might have thought he'd lain down for a nap. I stepped closer and the lights danced along my arms, but they didn't seem to have any effect on me. I gazed down on Caden's face and felt a familiar tug at my heart. He'd been so kind and gentle. I reached out to him and placed my hand on his hair.

Alarms sounded—long, drawn-out shrieks that I ignored as I bent and kissed him. Could I wake Caden just as the prince had awakened Sleeping Beauty? Apparently not, for as I leaned back, his eyes remained closed.

I waited beside him for the Nera to come in answer to the alarm. I didn't know if what I felt was resignation or anger. Whichever it was, it provided me with the strength I needed to face Nashira. I didn't take my eyes from Caden when footsteps scraped up the ladder.

"Wait here," Nashira said to someone outside. "So you've discovered our secret."

I turned to her. "How could you do this to your own son?"

"You couldn't hope to understand."

She wandered over and glanced at Caden before turning quickly away. "It pains me to have to do this to him, but I believe he'd agree with my reasons."

"You locked up Caden to save your own skin."

"I did it to protect the Nera from Tuldume and the growing power he wields. You must understand, he's already closed the outports and we can't do anything to stop him from coming into Nereen and controlling everything we've worked for. He needed Caden secured for a while. I'd have set him free once I dealt with Tuldume. One life for many." She dismissed me with the wave of her hand. "It doesn't matter what you think."

I got up and placed my palm on her arm and she stared, wide-eyed, at my hand.

"What power has Enrial given you now?"

"Let him go, Nashira. Even if the Major could destroy Nereen, what difference would it make? It's the end of your reign on Aten and it's time to go out there," I inclined my head toward the door, "out into the world and meet the people you've been avoiding ever since you came."

"Do you remember I once asked if you'd been sent here to destroy or help us? You promised you'd never destroy us."

"Think of it as being set free."

Lifting the hem of her long dress, she swept to the door and pointed to a lever hidden behind a wall brace. "Take him. It's what you're meant to do, isn't it?" Nashira gazed at Caden's face. "He'll never forgive me for this. He won't awaken for several days, but when he does, tell him I died."

I waited until the voices in the clearing were gone, proud of myself for not ripping Nashira's head off. She might not agree, but she was the evil queen as far as I was concerned. I reached up with both hands and pulled down the lever. The sparkling lights faded out and Caden's body floated to the floor.

I finally understood what the fortune-teller in Holo meant when she said I'd have to choose between light and dark. I'd thought I'd have to make the easy choice between good and evil, but she'd meant Caden and Rad. That decision wasn't so simple.

My hand fell away from the lever and, once again, I knelt beside Caden. He was absolutely beautiful, loyal and honest. He'd protected and loved me. I pressed my fists against my stomach, disgusted that I'd even imagined either choice could be mine. Caden would be with Catta and Rad with Stala. The fortune-teller was wrong—I didn't have to choose at all.

# Chapter Twenty-Five

The next morning, Heline and I strapped Caden onto a stretcher we'd rigged behind a small, black mare. I led the horse up the hill where Heline pointed out the invisible door in the equally invisible barrier. I pressed my palm in the air. The door slid aside, and the world outside Nereen flashed into view. I no longer had the necklace, but the snake-shaped welt gave me some power, while the charm, a melted lump of silver, would never take me home again. Juna waited on the other side of the barrier, her hands filled with bags.

"Take these supplies with you. I'd hate to think of you out there with nothing." Juna threw the bags over the horse. "She's not all bad, you know."

"No, she seems a fine horse." I climbed into the saddle.

Juna smiled. "I meant Nashira."

"If you say so."

"You'll need this as well." Juna reached into the folds of the blue cloak she wore and pulled out a dagger, sheathed in a glittering jeweled case.

"I don't want it," I said.

"Aten is unsafe, particularly for you."

"Even if I carried it with me, I'd never use it." I shook the reins and clicked my tongue. "Thank you, Juna."

I didn't look back. She'd probably have been lost from sight anyway, behind Nereen's barrier.

I felt nothing—my heart and soul were numb. Caden stayed in his dream world, looking as though he'd sleep away our last few days together. The grating of the stretcher's wheels over the ground was my only companion on the otherwise quiet morning.

I remembered the way to Ganodu from the time I'd traveled there with Caden, Neil and Aladar, and knew if I continued west through the Drylands, it would take only two or three days. I prayed Nashira was right and Caden wouldn't awaken until after I was long gone. I'd leave it to Catta to decide what to tell him—maybe she would say I'd died alongside Nashira.

The sun shimmered on the hot, sandy dunes, creating shadows and forms where none existed. Each time I spotted one of these ghosts, my hands tightened on the reins as I waited for Rad to appear above the rise. He never did, and part of me ached with the disappointment of knowing I might never see him again.

And that always brought me back to thoughts of what was in store for me. I couldn't return to my own home and time, yet there was nothing left here except the archive, and the thought of knocking around that stadium-sized museum all alone filled me with sadness. I'd be the keeper of technology and lost history, while the world outside struggled with the very basics of life. Alone, I could never hope to accomplish what Enrial wanted.

I'd named the mare Hometown, hoping, I suppose, that she'd take me there or someplace I could call my own. She was gentle and uncomplaining and had an uncanny ability to root out the smallest pool of water. When she did, I let her drink until her belly sloshed.

Hometown's head bobbed as she walked. I leaned forward and stroked her long neck, marveling how the late afternoon sun reflected off her deep, black coat.

"You're a good girl," I whispered.

She stopped and shook her head as though trying to dislodge a bothersome tick, so I slid down to give her ear a scratch. Then I saw what must've caught Hometown's attention.

A gray spiral of smoke rose over the next dune, its tendrils carrying the pleasant smell and sounds of sizzling food. Then a familiar, singsong voice followed by laughter. I searched my memory for the owner of the voice, but the information eluded me. Not sensing danger in the elusive memory, I led Hometown and Caden toward the mouth-watering smells and promise of human contact.

The little camp consisted of three horse-drawn carts, a covered wagon and a large fire surrounded by about ten people. They wore long, dull-brown cloaks with colorful leggings, pants and skirts peeking out beneath the hems.

I wasn't sure how to announce my presence, but after standing there for several moments, one of the women looked up, screamed and pointed. I held up my hands to show I was unarmed, but the men grabbed clubs.

"Lower your weapons." A tall man approached me, cocking his head to the side. "You look familiar."

The man with the singsong voice. I gazed down at his leggings, then at a cart filled with juggler's pins and balls.

"You helped my friend, Neil, and me escape from the guards in Holo."

He narrowed his eyes, not seeming convinced.

"For you, it was a long time ago," I said. "You were on your way to Atoll and dropped us by the Awes Forest."

His eyes lit and he grinned. "Of course, I remember now. We wondered what happened to the two of you." He waved his hand toward the rest of the group. "Please, come join us. Tell us your tale."

Hometown followed me down, dragging Caden behind her.

"Is he injured?" One of the women pointed to the stretcher.

"No, but he'll be asleep for a few days." I tethered my horse to the back of a cart, tidied Caden's blankets then stuck out my hand to the man. "I'm Jodi."

The troupe of acrobats, jugglers and dancers welcomed me as though I were a long-lost relative, sharing their food and the warmth of their fire. As dusk turned to night, I settled on one of the woolen throws scattered on the ground and allowed myself the luxury of imagining I belonged to the friendly group—just for tonight, I'd pretend I had somewhere to go. Each time they needled me for my story, I'd shake my head because I wouldn't even have known where to begin.

"Do stop, Gule, it's obvious she's not willing to share," said a woman and she nodded knowingly. "Though I'll bet she's got quite the tale to tell."

Behind me, the stairs leading from the covered wagon creaked. Turning, I glimpsed an unsteady foot tremble down on the top step.

"Let me help you, Auntie." Gule rushed toward the descending figure and grasped her elbow.

"Leave me be, boy, I've been up and down these steps more often than you've caught one of your pins." She waved her arms, not allowing Gule to touch her.

It was the blind fortune-teller from Holo. I rose up and backed away.

"We've a visitor," Gule said. He motioned me over. "Jodi, come meet Lurren."

The fortune-teller sniffed the air and zeroed in on me. Her eyebrows shot up. "So you survived?"

"You know one another?" Gule asked.

"She told me my fortune in Holo." I thought I should say something more. "She's very good."

"Have you made your decision yet?" Lurren approached me unaided and laid her cold, wrinkled hand on my arm.

"You mean between light and dark?" She nodded and I went on. "There's no decision to make because neither choice is available."

"You're wrong, child, the choice should be yours." Lurren held her palms to the fire and rubbed them together.

"I'm afraid I don't understand," I said.

"You're trying hard not to understand." She rolled her milky-white eyes and sighed. "Every choice you make impacts the outcome."

I looked at Gule, hoping he'd intervene, but he simply shrugged his shoulders.

"I've made the choice to settle for neither," I said.

"Then the choice will be made for you." Lurren clapped her hands. "It's too quiet here. Music, that's what we need."

Lying in the warm bedding Juna had provided, I tried to recall the last few hours, but it was only a whirl of colors and sounds—I'd been too lost in my own thoughts to enjoy the efforts of the jugglers and dancers. I'd made up my mind that Lurren's words had nothing to do with reality and she was simply a sideshow attraction.

Snores and rustling circulated around the camp. I closed my eyes; thankful I'd come upon the group so I'd not have to spend the night alone. I hadn't slept after finding Caden the night before and the lack of rest threatened to overwhelm me. I was safe here. My mind and body gave in and I floated into dreamland.

I traveled with Gule and the troupe until mid-day. We hugged and they wished me well, looks of concern on their faces. Lurren called me over to where she sat, ramrod straight, on the bench of the wagon.

"Give me your palm," she said.

I held out my left hand and smiled.

"You know the one I mean."

I sighed and raised the hand I'd been hiding behind my back.

"Ah," she said, running her fingers over the welt. "It's true then. I thought it was a trick you were playing."

"What is it?" I asked.

"A harbinger. I may be blind but can still read my cards. I saw it coming and, now, here it is." Lurren closed my fingers over my palm. "Keep it hidden, child. It's powerful, but may one day bring great sadness."

"I still don't know what you mean."

She laughed, sounding like a triumphant crow. "Oh, don't worry yourself. I'm just a poor, old woman—what would I know? Isn't that right, Gule? Let's get moving or we'll never make it to Syden."

I forced a grin onto my face and waved, but after they'd disappeared from sight, I let the tears come. My life was full of people coming and going—no one ever stayed. Rushing to Caden, I laid my wet cheek against his chest and, as always, the beating of his heart embraced me. Hometown stamped her hoof and tossed her mane. Unlike me, she must've been eager to be on her way. I stroked Caden's dark hair then mounted my horse, knowing the longer I was near him, the harder it would be to leave him in Ganodu.

By late afternoon, the fall colors of Ganodu's forests beckoned ahead. I pretended to enjoy the dappled leaves as I rode beneath them while, all the time, my gut twisted in a thousand different directions. Was this one of those forks in the road Lurren had spoken of? By going off without waiting for Caden to awaken, I'd never know what his decision would have been. Shouldn't I make him aware of his options?

I took a deep breath. No, he was needed here with Catta, to rebuild Ganodu. I wasn't. The road I had to take was entirely different. Lurren was right; I was making my choice.

The road was covered in orange and red leaves, dried and crunchy, making it impossible to hide the sound of my approach. Further on, I passed fields still filled with dying crops. The Dani had been unable to harvest while they searched for Caden—it would be a long winter for the tribe.

I waited by Ganodu's gates, noting that the village remained empty. They must have stayed in their makeshift home deeper in the forest. They would come for me, I was sure of it.

I slid from Hometown; not bothering to tether her, and stretched. I kept my gaze averted from Caden's motionless body, but it was no use; I needed to look one last time. I hurried to him and studied every bit of him—his copper-colored skin and the lids that hid his dark eyes. I wanted, so much, to hold him. I reached out my hand.

"You've found him!" Catta pushed me aside as she rushed to Caden.

I watched her cradle his head on her lap and stroke his cheek.

"What's wrong with him?"

"He'll be all right in a few days, or so I was told." I stepped back and searched, unseeing, for the reins behind me. "Take good care of him, Catta."

"You're leaving?"

"I've got to go."

She stood and walked slowly toward me. "It's not like you to give up so easily."

"I'll always fight for what is rightfully mine." I pulled myself onto the horse, a difficult task since my body was sapped of all feeling. "Unfortunately, I don't know what's mine anymore."

Before she could say anything more, I leaned forward and gave a ferocious kick to Hometown's sides. The poor horse looked back at me, her eyes wide, and then took off along the road toward the Hachi's Forest.

# Chapter Twenty-Six

I leaned far over Hometown's neck, urging her to go faster. Her hooves pounded the dirt road, the heavy beat matching the thumping in my heart. All the worries and emotions of the past week closed in on me and I was sure if I went fast enough, I could escape them. Hometown's gasps for breath brought me back to reality and I pulled on the reins, allowing the poor thing to slow. After she'd cooled down, I dismounted and stroked her velvety nose, apologizing for the harsh kick I'd given her. She seemed to forgive me and nuzzled my hand.

A tapping intruded into my thoughts and I looked around. The Hachi Forest stretched below us, at the bottom of a steep hill. I picked up the reins and led Hometown along the top of the rise, letting the setting sun warm my face. I hated the thought of sleeping alone so near the Hachi, but they never ventured from under the trees. At least, I hoped they didn't. Unwilling to take the chance, I led Hometown away from the spiders' home to the forest that blanketed the other side of the hill. I assumed this area belonged to the Dani and would be relatively safe.

By the time I'd found a suitable clearing, the sky was dark and the air had turned a bone chilling cold. I ate the dried fruit

Juna had packed and, unwilling to build a fire, went to bed early. My mind skipped from Caden to Lurren's final words. Nothing she said made sense. But the truth was, I didn't want it to make sense because, if it did, it would be just one more thing I'd need to fear. After a few minutes of listening to the owls hooting, I pulled the covers over my head and wished the night away.

I watched the entrance to the archive all afternoon. No one seemed to be around, but that meant nothing. The Major could easily use his brooch in the same manner I'd used the charm to travel and he might appear out of nowhere if I slipped through the opening. Without the charm, I wasn't even sure I could open the elevator to the archive.

I'd left Hometown on the other side of the forest, munching happily on the grass there. It had taken me longer to travel by foot, but I figured the meadow would have been far too tempting to the hungry horse and she'd have given away our presence. I sat back, ripping apart a brittle leaf I'd picked up from the ground and thought about my options.

I could go back for the horse and rush for the entrance. The problem was, I had no idea if speed would make any difference. I had the feeling that if the Major wanted to stop me, he'd have no problem at all. Again I tried envisioning the inside of the archive, wondering if I needed the charm to travel around Aten. It appeared I did because I was still sitting in the forest and the archive was out of reach.

There was another option, but I wasn't sure I could pull it off. If I did, it wouldn't matter if the Major waited for me by the elevator. I could use my ability to injure him. But it wasn't so simple because I wasn't sure it worked against the Nera and their kind. I had a feeling that Enrial might have put some restrictions on it. I threw down the scrap of leaf I still held, got up then headed back the way I'd come. When it came down to it, there was only one way for me to ever have any peace on Aten. I'd have to steal the brooch from the Major.

There were three ways to the canyon and the Chuma Pass was out of the question. I wasn't sure I'd find the entrance to the Illusion Pass on this side of the hills, so that left going around the Jagger Hills. It added an extra three or four days to my trip, but time was something I had a lot of.

The nights were the worst. I could shut out the darkness and the spooky noises, but I couldn't turn off my thoughts. I wondered if Rad and Stala were back in Kopi. In my head I saw them side-by-side, digging into the past. Perhaps Chowder watched them from a lofty perch. Occasionally they might wonder what happened to me. Stala would say I'd probably married Caden and Rad would comment that it was all for the best. I woke up sure the vision was taking place right in front of me, only to find Hometown and a faint rising sun.

I didn't meet anyone else as I traveled and, reaching the lower heights of the Jagger Hills, I easily passed over them. By that time I figured I was only a few days from Holo and I still hadn't come up with a plan to steal the brooch from the Major.

As Hometown plodded along the steep path leading into Deakin Canyon, my breath sent gray puffs into the cold air. Winter had settled between the colorful canyon walls and I didn't look forward to the lonely trip I had ahead of me. Truth was, I didn't know the route to Holo through the canyon. I planned to head to the canyon's east side, knowing the Awes Forest was at the top. If I stayed close, it would eventually lead me where I needed to go. What I didn't count on was the winding canyon trails that never went in a straight line. By the end of the first day, I was lost.

I tried not to panic, reassuring myself that I could leave the canyon by any one of the paths that normally marked the walls.

Unfortunately, I never came across the paths or the river. I tried using the sun to direct me south, but after following a trail for more than an hour, I discovered I'd somehow got turned around and faced north.

I unrolled my bedding beside the spot I'd tied up Hometown. She'd found a little puddle of water and slurped it almost as though she knew we might be in for some dry times. Clutching the blanket, I decided tomorrow I'd let Hometown take me wherever she wanted—chances were her choices would be better than mine. Pleased with my decision, I fell asleep to the comforting sound of my horse's swishing tail.

The following morning, I dropped the reins over Hometown's neck and let her wander. With her head bobbing, she meandered along the dusty paths, never pausing when she reached a fork in the road. There was a chance I might not end up in Holo, but it was one I was willing to take; I didn't want to spend another icy night in the canyon. I kept my blanket wrapped around my shoulders and dug my chin into my chest. About midday, hunger set in and I pulled Hometown to a stop. I slid down and that's when I heard the noise.

I stood, gripping the reins in my hand and holding my breath. I waited for the sound again, hoping I'd only imagined it. I hadn't. The rasp of another horse's hooves echoed around the bend then stopped. Whoever it was must've realized I was no longer moving. I tried getting back into the saddle without it making its usual creaking leather noise. Fine gravel slid beneath my feet and skittered across the path. I froze, poised halfway up. My arms cramped and when I could no longer stand it, I jumped on Hometown, shook the reins and we took off.

I could no longer hear the other horse following behind, but I was sure it was still there and it didn't take much brainpower to recognize the danger. Someone was tracking me and they might be looking for more than a little companionship. My mind swept over the possibilities: Chuma, the Major's soldiers, or some other threat I'd not yet had the pleasure of meeting.

I leaned over Hometown's neck. It didn't surprise me when she flew around a bend and skidded to a halt by the river. Hometown may not have been good at finding a path out of the canyon, but she aced finding water. The Deakin River rushed below us; we'd never survive crossing it. My shoulders slumped and I turned her around. Was I willing to use my ability against whom—or whatever followed me? Like a traffic cop on a busy intersection, I raised my palm in front of me. Did the snake-shaped welt have more power than merely opening doors?

# Chapter Twenty-Seven

The tumbling river hid the sounds of whoever approached. My imagination bounced off the rainbow-colored canyon walls and by the time a horse nosed around the bend, I was almost ready to dive into the water and take my chances there.

"Don't freak out, I know you're pissed off."

I plunged my shaking hand behind me. "You scared the hell out of me, Neil. How long have you been following me?"

"About two days." He jumped from his horse, never taking his gaze from my face. "You may as well have carried a neon sign on your head; you're lousy at covering your tracks."

"I wasn't aware I needed to." I turned away, unsure how I was supposed to react. "What are you doing here?"

"Where else am I supposed to go? A bit of an unwanted guest around here, aren't I?"

I faced him. "That's your own fault."

"Everyone makes mistakes." He'd dressed in layers and looked much larger than I knew he actually was.

"You've shaved off your beard and cut your hair," I said.

"Yeah, great disguise, huh?" He ran his dirty fingers over his chin. "You look tired."

"A lot's happened." I stared at him. "What you did was really stupid."

"You're right." He dropped his reins and took a step closer to me. "We can stand here all day and discuss what an idiot I am, or you can forgive me."

"There's another option. I could tell you to leave."

"Do you want me to?" He blinked and angled his head to the side.

"Why did you team up with Arax?"

"Dad gave up on the archive, but I just couldn't—it's all I could think about. Then one day, in Atoll, I met up with Arax and he seemed to want to help Aten's progress as much as I did." Neil sighed. "I was desperate."

"I don't know how or why Arax would've done anything to help," I said.

"He said Caden might be able to open it with his voice."

"Caden would never do that."

He nodded then gazed around. "This path is a dead end."

"That's pretty obvious. How do I get out of here?"

"Depends on where you want to go."

I looked over my shoulder at the swirling water. It seemed years since we'd first entered this canyon, prisoners of the Dani. Back then, Neil and I had held onto each other for comfort, knowing we could depend on one another. Aten had changed him, yet I had to believe my best friend still lurked somewhere behind those blue eyes. I didn't know if I could forgive him, but I'd have to trust him again. No, it was more than that—I needed to trust him. I needed a friend. Turning, I stared into his eyes—eyes full of sadness and a silent plea. I made up my mind and, right or wrong, told him about the brooch and my plan to steal it.

"You're right, it's the only way you'll ever be safe," Neil said. He led us back the way we'd come, promising to get me to Holo in two days.

"I was in Nereen, but I didn't see your dad." I stuck a twig into the fire and watched as the sparks flew into the early evening sky. "Didn't you say he was there?"

"Could be back in Kopi by now."

Kopi. That's where Rad was with Stala. And here were Neil and I, destined to be outsiders forever.

"Just how do you plan on getting the brooch from the Major? He must take it wherever he goes," Neil said. "And I don't see you walking up to him and taking it off his chest."

"Haven't given it much thought, but I'll never be safe from him as long as he has it."

We'd camped atop the western edge of the Deakin Canyon. The Awes Forest, far on the other side, was filled with lush, almost tropical looking trees while this forest brimmed with shadowy cedars and pine trees. Neil rose up from where he lay beside the fire and threw on more wood.

"I'll help you."

"Are you sure?" I held my breath, hoping he'd say yes.

"I owe you one." He glanced at my neck. "You lost the necklace again?"

"It's gone forever, just a big lump of silver now." I explained what had happened in Nereen.

"It's probably for the best. Aten isn't ready for technology."

"You're not disappointed that you might never get into the archive again?" I asked.

"Amazing, huh? After all this time and everything I did to try and get in." He shrugged and rested against the coiled rope and saddlebags he'd taken from his horse.

"Maybe I can still open the archive." I paused then showed him my palm. "With this, I can open any door, any lock."

He leaned forward, stared at the welt then shook his head. "Don't even tempt me, Jodi. Anyway, there's a lot more of Aten I want to see."

We didn't speak for a few minutes, the crackle of the fire accentuating the silence.

"Remember I said I'd made the right decision in staying here?" Neil asked. I nodded and he continued. "Lately, I couldn't even picture what it was like before Aten. When I saw you at the Nera's camp, the memories came flooding back and it scared me because I knew everything I was doing here was wrong and you'd hate me for it. Being in this place is a death sentence and I would give anything to go back home with you."

I swallowed, but didn't know what to say. The truth was, I would give anything to go back home with him—back to the way things used to be.

\*   \*   \*   \*

The next evening, we stared down at Holo—an unwelcome sight that was becoming far too familiar. Neil and I hadn't talked again about the choices he'd made while on Aten, but I knew he was feeling the burden of it. I pulled him back to the campsite we'd set up.

"Before we go down there, I've got to tell you something." I blinked away tears. "You're my best friend and I do forgive you."

Neil nodded and wrapped his arms around me. I felt moisture on my forehead where he leaned his cheek.

"Thank you," he whispered. After a few moments, he pulled away. "Now let me tell you what I have planned for Holo."

It was nearing midnight. The lights of Holo wavered and dimmed as the cold winds swept over the quiet town. Using small pieces of burned firewood, Neil and I had smeared charcoal onto our faces. We'd giggled so hard you'd have thought we were having our faces painted at a fair. It wasn't until we'd crept through the darkness to the edge of town that the seriousness of the situation touched my heart.

"I'm scared." I licked the bitter charcoal from my lips.

Neil grabbed my hand. "Why don't I get the brooch for you?"

"No, I've got to make sure it's there and if it is, I want to get it." It would have been so nice to hand the job over to Neil, but I couldn't. Despite having told him differently, I still wasn't sure I could trust him. "What makes you think anything in this town will burn? It's made out of earth and bricks."

"This wooden barrier will make a pretty big bonfire to start. If I can get on the other side, I'll see what else will burn in this rat-infested place." He let go of my hand. "Let's go."

The deep, spike-filled ditch that circled Holo had always intrigued me, but I never imagined I'd be getting such a close look at it. Puffs of dust followed us as we slid into the ditch , far from the gates on either side.

"I'll go around to the other side." Neil pointed along the ditch to some unseen spot. "You get as close as you can to the gatepost. When the guards see the fire on the other side, they're sure to investigate. That's when you sneak in."

"Neil, wait."

"What is it?"

"Meet you by the camp, okay?"

"Jodi, when you get the brooch, go back to the camp, get on your horse and get out of here. Don't wait for me." He bent and kissed my cheek. "Promise me."

"I promise," I whispered. "You too, okay?"

He nodded. "Good luck." Neil ran, hunched over and was lost in the darkness of the ditch.

I crept on my hands and knees, afraid the coiled rope Neil had given me might be visible from above. When I was as close to the guards as I dared, I slipped the rope to the side, rolled onto my back and stared at the stars.

The very first night Neil and I had been on Aten, I'd been amazed by the multitude and brightness of the stars. The crisp, cold air seemed to make them even more so. If I wasn't success-ful in finding and escaping with the brooch, I might never see this or any other sky again. I searched for a familiar constellation and waited.

When I heard a distant yell, I jumped up and slung the rope over my shoulder, careful not to stab myself with the large hook we'd tied to one end. Still in the ditch, I ran to the road leading past the guardhouse and peered over the top. The coast was clear—the guards and soldiers must have rushed to the other side of town, investigating the fire Neil had set. I scrambled to the road and dashed into the market, the only way to the interior buildings of Holo. The place still smelled of sweat and grease, even though everyone must have left hours before. I dove down the side street that led into the square outside the Major's house; the square where Neil and I had been auctioned. Confused yells hopped over the buildings, but I saw no one as I turned the corner into the cobbled square. I stopped, took a quick look around, and then crept under the torch-lit windows of the Major's lair.

As I leaned back and twirled the hook at the end of the rope, I heard the sound of quick marching feet and assumed the Major's soldiers were now seeing to the fire. The hook landed on the inside of one of the hallway windows, but the clunk of metal hardly made a dent in a silence broken by the calls and yells of people awakening.

I hadn't expected to do so well throwing and landing the hook. I bit my lip, wondering if I'd used up all my luck in my first five minutes. I shrugged and started climbing. Pressing my feet against the brick, I was grateful the Awes' boots didn't slip. Clambering up to the opening on the third-story, I concentrated on putting one hand above the other and each foot in the little crevices between the bricks.

I gripped the window ledge with my fingers, resting for a second before pulling myself over. It was quiet in the tower, so perhaps the Major was away. As wonderful as that sounded, I hoped it wasn't true because where the Major went, I was sure the brooch followed.

I tiptoed down the long hallway to the closed, wooden doors and leaned my ear against one, listening for any movement or sound. Nothing. Would the brooch still be in the silver box on his table? I wiped my damp palms on my pants and grasped the doorknob. It turned and I pulled.

"Most people entering Holo, do so with far less fanfare." The Major sat behind the table, raising a roasted chicken to his mouth.

I stepped back, but knew it was no use as he stood and dipped his oily fingers into the silver box, lifting the brooch from its nest.

# Chapter Twenty-Eight

The twinkling brooch looked small on the Major's immense chest; a tiny treasure hidden in a vast desert. I couldn't help myself—I walked across the red tiles and waited in his shadow.

"I became very ill the last time you were here and missed our date at the archive." He came from behind the table and raised his arm, letting the fake necklace and charm I'd given him swing from his fingers. "I've a feeling it wasn't our date that brought you back. What have you in mind?"

"I...I'll take you to the archive."

How was I going to get out of here? I tore my gaze away from the brooch and focused on his eyes. I'd never noticed how round and bland they were.

"Just like that?"

Black smoke crept through the window and across the room, but the Major ignored it.

I licked my lips and edged toward him. "I don't care about the archive anymore, you can have it. I just want to get it over with so you'll leave me alone."

"Won't Enrial be disappointed that her protégé has no interest in helping Aten?" He leaned forward and gripped my neck.

"You'll be my little assistant from now on and there is nothing Enrial can do to help you."

He drew my face close to his own. The toxic smell of whatever burned below the window tore at my throat and I tried to cough, but his fingers squeezed harder. I'd been afraid to mention the brooch to Enrial; afraid she'd take it from the Major and use it to control me. Now I wished I had told her. The Major grinned and his fingers loosened. Keeping my gaze on his bulbous face and lifting the sides of my mouth in what I hoped was a smile, I slowly raised my arm. The brooch took the Major anywhere he wanted to go, would it take me?

"I need to get out of here." My hand darted to his chest, curled my fingers around the icy brooch and tore it away. I stumbled back thinking of the campsite, the archive, the market—anything. But nothing happened.

He laughed and moved toward me. "How far do you think you'll get with that?"

I fled to the hall and down the same stairs that Juna and I had taken to the market only days ago, not caring that I couldn't see the steps in front of me. The fire Neil had set must have drawn the guards away from their posts, for none were stationed along the unlit stairs. The Major's heavy footsteps sounded on the stone floor behind me.

The staircase ended and I lost my footing, landing face first into the wall. I brushed the grit away with the back of my hand and felt moisture that I guessed had to be blood. I started to push myself up with the other hand when I realized I'd dropped the brooch and kneeling, swept the dark floor with my palms. I couldn't find it!

The scrape of the Major descending the stairs squeezed the breath out of me and I choked back the sobs. Where was the brooch?

"You haven't the skill to use it," he said, his voice circling me like a hungry panther. "Give it to me."

I imagined him with his hand out—patient and sure that I'd meekly give him what he wanted. I backed against the wall, trying to press myself into the rock.

"Come now, let's stop playing these childish games." His foot raked over another step.

I didn't care about the brooch and only wanted out. I crawled away from his gravelly voice, one tiny bit at a time, but with each movement, he came closer, his steps sounding like a shovel piercing the hard ground beneath me. Gathering my last bit of courage, I crouched, placing my hands on either side as though waiting for the starter's pistol, and I touched on the icy shape of the brooch.

Closing my hand around it, I tried again to envision the campsite where Neil and I had left our things. The jagged edge of the brooch dug into my skin and a frustrated cry escaped my lips.

The weight of the Major's hand dropped onto my shoulder and I twisted away, but his fingers closed around the back of my clothes and he pulled me against him.

"Let me go!"

He laughed again and his hot breath poured over my neck. I squirmed and jabbed him with my elbow. I didn't encounter the soft flab I'd expected; his massive mounds of flesh were solid muscle. The Major grappled with his free hand, almost pulling my arm from its socket as he reached for the brooch. His fist crushed mine. My knees buckled and I slid to the floor, my arm dangling above me from the stranglehold the Major had on my hand. A wave of exhaustion washed over me—whatever strength I'd had was almost gone, yet I still held onto the brooch. If only I could have found the door, I might have made it to the market.

The dim light of the stars and moon over the market blinded me after the dark stairway. The Major's hold suddenly loosened and I sprang away, tripping then gaining my feet once more. The brooch had worked! I looked over my shoulder, dismayed to see that because the Major had been touching me, he'd been transported to the market as well. The lumps on his face ballooned and he came at me, his cobra-like arm striking out.

I leapt away from him then turned and started running, trying to figure out why the brooch had worked. What had changed since I'd first tried it? Was it because the Major had been holding it as well? Or was it something else? I couldn't think straight while the Major chased me, calling to the guards who dotted the market. How the hell had I made it work?

Racing toward the gate, I spotted the guards barring my way. There was no escape. I stopped as they started toward me. Twenty meters. I needed to think. I needed to relax. Relax! I'd been drained of all my strength and will to fight when the brooch had whisked us to the market. I needed to relax.

Before the guards pounced, a thousand thoughts whirled through my head: Breathe deep, soft music, a walk in the park, a soothing bath…go to the campsite for Neil.

The guards, the market and the Major disappeared, but so had Neil, his horse and gear. Our campsite was deserted, and only the bag containing our food teetered on top of a rock as though placed there only seconds before. I stared at the neatly arranged bundle, hoping Neil might have simply forgotten it and would return at any moment. The brooch had saved me, but instead of the elation I'd expected, I felt as though someone was squeezing the last bit of hope from my heart. Finally, I slung the bag over Hometown before pulling myself into the saddle. I couldn't wait around—the Major and his men would surely search even though they wouldn't know where the brooch had taken me.

I still held the brooch in my hand. I longed to use it, yet I was afraid its power would betray me. I opened the bag, stuffed the brooch into the bottom and then turned Hometown toward the western edge of the canyon—opposite the Awes Forest. The elation of my victory over the Major turned to misery. I'd never see Neil again.

I seldom took the blanket from around my shoulders as Hometown and I moved northward along the edge of Deakin Canyon. No one followed us. The Major would never be able to pop up in the middle of nowhere without the brooch. For a while I'd be safe.

The future of Aten weighed heavily on my mind. Opening the archive to the people here would cause more problems than solutions. I agreed with Neil—Aten wasn't ready for technology. Not yet. I could've gone south to find warmer weather before winter set in, but I needed some sense of home, even if home had disappeared hundreds of years before. After traveling for two days, snow fell . But even worse, I was running out of food. It seemed I could never stop shivering. Then, on the third day, I spotted the tops of the Jagger Hills gleaming like snow cones in the distance.

That night, sheltered under an outcrop of rock on one side and Hometown on the other, I pulled out my last bit of food from the bag Neil had given me. Along with the crumbs at the bottom, I felt something else.

Trembling, I pulled out a small bundle wrapped in a ragged bit of cloth. Opening it, I discovered my journal, charred around the edges and still holding a pencil in its spiral binding. A loose page fluttered onto my lap and I recognized Neil's handwriting.

*Dear Jodi*

*I found your journal in the fire pit near Paul's body. I meant to return it to you sooner, but I wanted to read your poems one last time. Remember you used to read them to me? I know it's impossible for you to forget what a jerk I've been, but I swear I never did anything other than listen to Arax's ideas.*

*If I still could, I'd dream us out of this place—back home where there is no magic, no archive and no Arax. If you go to Kopi, I know you'll be safe with my Dad.*

*Your friend (always), Neil*

I placed the letter carefully into the journal and flipped through the pages. The only page missing was the map to the archive, probably taken by Arax. Everything else was there. I clutched it against my chest, wondering why Neil and I had willingly left those good times behind.

It took me two hungry days to find the Illusion Pass. Before going in, I let Hometown nibble on the grass she uncovered with her nose and hoof. My stomach rumbled and gurgled as I melted snow in a pan over the fire. As long as I drank water, I'd be okay, though that knowledge didn't banish the hunger pangs.

Even sheltered from the bitter wind, the air nipped at my face as Hometown and I squeezed along the narrow path. I'd wrapped cloths around my hands, but they did little to protect my fingers from the numbing cold.

When we broke through the passage, I wasn't surprised to see an open patch of grass where the pond had been. A single tree grew from its center, the autumn leaves still clinging to its branches. Hometown tugged on the rein and I watched as she bent her head and ripped up chunks of the green shoots.

I walked around the tree, my neck bent back. I'd never seen leaves shaped like those—huge, elephant ears, curled at the edges, and the smooth trunk looked as though someone had stripped away the bark. I wondered why Neil and I had seen something different. How was it decided what illusion each person would see?

I pulled everything from Hometown's back and let her wander across the small island of grass. She whinnied and I heard her slurping merrily away. Sure enough, when I bounded over to where she stood on the far side of the clearing, a small stream gurgled.

Oddly enough, the Illusion Pass didn't frighten me now. It could have been because it was the place Enrial had visited, but I wasn't sure. Perhaps I sensed a bubble of safety surrounded it. I followed the stream, crossing over a small wooden bridge. On the other side, another patch of green spread out with a fire blazing in its center. There wasn't anyone there—there wasn't any place they could have hidden because all around me, the walls of the Jagger Hills reached straight up.

A pot simmered to one side of the fire on top of a layer of hot coals. A ladle stuck out from the pot and I picked it up with my cloth-wrapped hands. I hesitated for only a moment before bringing the contents to my lips.

By the time it was dark, the pot was empty and I'd set up my bedding beside the now red coals. My full stomach hurt in the most wonderfully drowsy way. Hometown and I could stay here forever if we needed to.

The next morning, I awoke covered in snow. The only thing visible was the tree on the far side, and with its leaves gone, it stood like a gray shadow of its former self. Hometown waited quietly as I piled my belongings onto her. I was glad she'd been able to share my illusion and enjoy a long overdue meal.

It wasn't until I was almost at the archive that I admitted where I was going. I couldn't go to Ganodu, Kopi, Nereen or Windore; all those places held reminders of people who couldn't or wouldn't be a part of my life. How could I bring more pain to those who'd befriended me and helped me? I would have to look elsewhere for the safe haven Enrial had spoken of.

The meadow leading to the archive was a river of white; the snow extending far as the early afternoon sunshine glinted off its surface. Hometown's step quickened—she seemed to sense that the end of our journey was near. I patted her neck, encouraging her around the final bend. As I scanned the hills for the opening to the archive, I spotted a riderless horse. Too far away, I didn't recognize the beast. I swallowed and wondered what I ought to do because whoever it was, must've been inside the cave by the elevator.

My cold fingers twisted the reins. There was nowhere else for me to go, so I clicked my tongue, and Hometown eagerly sprinted forward. Nearing, I recognized the other horse and my heart crashed against my chest. We slowed and I could barely get down without falling. Good news or bad, I couldn't wait to get inside. I slipped down the passage and, bursting into the cavern, I couldn't help but smile.

He leaned against the far wall, cleaning his nails with a knife—Gramps' knife. My knapsack lay at his feet, a glint of green moss on its canvas surface.

Although I only wanted to be wrapped in the comfort of his arms, I asked, "How did you find it, Rad?"

"I told you I was the finder of lost possessions." He flipped the knife closed and handed it to me. "A little side trip into the Phosphor Caves."

"Why are you here?"

"Seems I've lost something and I wondered if you could help me find it." He arched his eyebrow.

"What?"

"You." He strode across the few feet that separated us and held my shoulders.

"I thought you and Stala..."

"Stala is like a sister to me and I a brother to her." Rad smiled and pulled me close. "It's been like that since the beginning."

I remembered the conversation I'd overheard between Stala and Rad outside the Phosphor Caves. I pressed my face into his chest, drinking in the shock of his touch.

"Then you've found what was lost." My voice was muffled against him. "And it won't be so easy to lose me again."

Rad and I rode our horses, side-by-side, in the middle of the meadow. Chowder, brushed and gleaming, purred in my lap. The cold no longer bothered me, nor did the long trip we had ahead of us to Windore.

"You're sure you don't want to go into the archive?" he asked again.

"One day I'm going to have to go in." I reached across the space between our horses and took his hand, delighting in the current that ran between us. "For now, I'm going to concentrate on my own future and let Aten take care of itself."

The End

# About the Author

Lynn Sinclair lives north of Toronto in Ontario, Canada with her husband, daughter and two cats. The surrounding forests filled with winding paths and fields dotted with grazing horses were her inspiration for the sometimes frightening, yet always beautiful world of Aten. Lynn is currently working on Jodi's next adventure.

# Chapter One of Lynn Sinclair's
# KEY TO ATEN
## the first Chronicle of Aten

The back door latch slipped into place without a sound. I closed my eyes and took a deep breath of freedom. The day was mine. Mom would call out to me, her words slurred even at this hour. She'd give up after a while and vow to give me hell. By the time I got home she'd forget why she was angry, but that wouldn't stop her nagging.

My fingers curled around my journal. I'd write today—my thoughts, poems and...my mood dipped as I remembered the haunting images I'd been having lately. No, I wouldn't let anything ruin this day.

Where to? Not the mall or coffee shop—all my friends had summer jobs there, jobs I couldn't take because I was forced to stick around and make sure Mom didn't set the house on fire. I was the only sixteen-year-old girl in town who wasn't working. I headed toward the forest where only the trees could crowd me.

It was nine o'clock and already hot outside. Down the street, Mrs. Moran's sprinkler washed over the thirsty grass. I stopped in front of her house, spread my arms wide and stood under the water as it spilled over the sidewalk. The cold drizzle streamed onto my head, then my face and finally my outstretched arms. I remembered the journal still clutched in my hand and dove out from under the drops. Shaking the water from my hair, I walked along the dirt path that led into the forest. The earthy smell of rotting leaves filled the air.

As always, I stopped under the towering oak, its limbs stretching over my head. Neil Moran and I had built a fort here when we were little. The tree was still strong enough to hold some old boards, a rope ladder and the memories shared by two kids. All those things were gone except the memories. Good times. Then about three years ago Neil had started acting strange, pulling away. I could still remember the ache in my stomach from the brush-off.

I moved on, following the trail to the top of a hill. Below, a narrow creek cut a path through the rippling, green meadow, the water bubbling over stones and splashing into a glistening pond. Piles of rocks and old cedar fences marked boundaries of long-gone fields. I'd always imagined having my house here—each day I could look out on the uninhabited world below. Sometimes you might see horses, their long necks arched as they ate. Today, there was only me.

I circled a large boulder, shade dappling its surface, and almost tripped over a pair of long legs splayed out over the ground. I looked down and there was Neil. His eyes were closed and his breath had that tiny, satisfied sound you make when you're totally relaxed. I'd rarely seen him these past three years, and whenever I did, he'd glance away. Sleeping, he looked as innocent as he did when we were six years old. Back then I was the new kid in the neighbourhood, teased about my red hair and freckles. Neil had never teased me.

I bent down, placed my journal on the boulder, and noticed the purple and green bruises on his arms. I reached out my hand, then hesitated. Should I wake him? Neil seemed happy enough to sleep the day away, but it would be great to talk to him—it had been so long. And I was curious about the bruises. I stretched out my arm and grasped his shoulder.

The world shook. The tree beside me slipped away, dissolving and sinking. The ground sucked at my legs and pulled me in. I clutched the boulder, but it was sinking as well. As the dirt and mud lapped around my shoulders, I looked frantically for Neil, but he was gone, just a few wisps of his blond hair poked up through the grass. I screamed his name and the muck came rushing in.

"What are you doing here, Jodi?" asked a bewildered voice.

I opened my eyes. Neil stood over me, his hands on his hips. No dirt clung to his clothes—I must've imagined the whole thing. I sat up, but the world continued to swirl. Sweat trickled into my eyes and I tucked my head between my upraised knees.

"I don't know what happened, it was horrible. I must've blacked out."

"How'd you get in my dream?"

"It was like the world was swallowing me up. And you, too." I shuddered.

"It's always like that—you get used to it," he said.

"I've got to go home."

"You can't, at least not until I wake up."

"What are you talking about? I want to go home." I tried to stand up.

He knelt down and placed his hand on my leg. "Take a look around. We aren't anywhere near home."

I looked. We were atop a hill, but not the one we'd been on moments before. Instead of grassy meadows, a sea of trees covered in white, shimmering lace lay below us. Far beyond that, a row of hills dotted the horizon. Behind us, a narrow dirt road ran through a thick forest of green that stretched across the landscape. No pond, no fences—no way home.

"Where are we?" I twisted my necklace.

Neil looked around. "I don't know, never been here."

**KEY TO ATEN**
**ISBN: 0974648175    $8.95    At your favorite bookstore**